All I

WANT FOR

Christmas

also by
Michelle Dykman

Her Sanctuary, His Heart

You, Me, and the Stars
BETHEL PRIVATE SCHOOL SERIES | BOOK ONE

Someone Like You
BETHEL PRIVATE SCHOOL SERIES | BOOK TWO

You Found Me
BETHEL PRIVATE SCHOOL SERIES | BOOK THREE

If Only In My Dreams
A SNOWY SPRINGS ROMANCE | BOOK ONE

The Deal With Dakota
A SNOWY SPRINGS ROMANCE | BOOK TWO

All I

WANT FOR

Christmas

A SNOWY SPRINGS ROMANCE

MICHELLE DYKMAN

AMBASSADOR INTERNATIONAL
GREENVILLE, SOUTH CAROLINA & BELFAST, NORTHERN IRELAND

www.ambassador-international.com

All I Want for Christmas

Paperback ISBN: 978-1-64960-512-2
eISBN: 978-1-64960-555-9

Cover design by Hannah Linder Designs
Interior Typesetting by Dentelle Design
Edited by Katie Cruice Smith

Scripture taken from the Holy Bible, New International Version®, NIV® Copyright ©1973, 1978, 1984, 2011 by Biblica, Inc.® Used by permission. All rights reserved worldwide.

AMBASSADOR INTERNATIONAL
Emerald House
411 University Ridge, Suite B14
Greenville, SC 29601, USA
www.ambassador-international.com

AMBASSADOR BOOKS
The Mount
2 Woodstock Link
Belfast, BT6 8DD, Northern Ireland, UK
www.ambassadormedia.co.uk

The colophon is a trademark of Ambassador, a Christian publishing company.

Therefore, if anyone is in Christ, the new creation has come:

The old has gone, the new is here!

2 Corinthians 5:17

To my dear friend Linda Hassell, I wish I had met you sooner.

Chapter One

"What in the . . . ." Noah Thomas stumbled, bracing himself against a nearby wall as his feet threatened to land him on his behind. Careful to move his prosthetic left leg into the correct position under him, he stabilized it with his right, regaining his balance. A dull throb in his right hand let him know of the collision with a brick wall to his left, which he'd used to break his fall.

Muttering harshly under his breath, he glanced down at his reddened palm. No damage there. He grimaced; he should have been watching where he was walking, noticing too late the frozen puddle of water under his feet. Without thinking, he curled his left hand into a fist, crushing the small piece of pastel colored paper stored there, barely taking note of the jagged edges. The paper was already heavily handled, it edges worn and torn. He should throw it away. Its presence only served as a reminder of all he had lost and the reason his attention had not been on the icy sidewalk. It had been eight months; he knew what it said by heart.

The slip of paper held two words. No name, no date.

I'm sorry.

Those were the last two words between him and his wife as their marriage imploded. Teneal, his first love and his bride, hadn't needed to sign her name; he knew her handwriting, just the same way he knew how she drank her coffee—black with two sugars—the way she smelled like coconut and roses, and the way she always ate her waffles soft instead of hard and crusty. All the things a husband should know about his wife. And yet somehow, he had missed the most important thing of all—the fact that she was unhappy.

Another heavy breath puffed from his chest. It was sharp, like the pain inside somehow would escape with it. It didn't. The hurt lingered, tightening the already strained muscles of his chest. Their soreness was a result of his new way of life, the adjustments he'd had to make. Time had not eased the sting of their parting; and the Christmas season, Teneal's favorite, only served to make the memories more prominent in his mind.

He opened his tight fist, staring down at the paper again. Why did he still carry it? To relive the pain of that night again and again? To remember her and the way she'd torn out his heart? No, that wasn't the reason. He knew why, and the knowledge hurt just like each time the reality of her death hit him. *It was your fault.*

His guilt would not allow him to forget; no matter how much time had passed, that one fact remained. It was his fault Teneal was gone, his fault she'd been out that night eight months ago, his fault the accident happened. He rubbed a work-roughened hand over his chin, feeling the start of new growth there. Teneal had loved his five-o clock shadow, had giggled when it rubbed her cheeks as he kissed her. He pushed the memory away. He should shave; or he should grow out his beard, so the memory of her kisses would no longer bother him.

Dumping the paper into his pocket, the abused muscles in his chest finally easing, he drew a steadying breath, careful to navigate around the icy puddles of the sidewalk. The prosthesis creaked slightly as he moved. Another memento of that night and a constant reminder that he could not return to a life he had once loved—a life he would once have died for and, in the end, the life that had cost him Teneal.

Boy, he was all sunbeams and joy today. Maybe it had something to do with the lack of sunlight, he mused. He replaced his woolen hat on his head and dug his hands into his jacket pockets for warmth.

"Noah?" his brother, Michael Thomas, called from somewhere behind him. Noah paused, settling his expression into what he hoped was a friendly smile.

"You're heading the wrong way." Michael laughed, coming alongside him.

"Which way am I supposed to be going?" He'd meant the words to come out less severe than they did; however, with thoughts as dark as his, they inevitably would be given voice. Michael took no notice.

Noah's return to Snowy Springs after his accident had been sudden and met by his parents with disbelief and compassion. They had to know that living in the same place where he and Teneal had built a life would slowly drive him mad. They didn't need to know what he was hiding. To him, perhaps the place where he had grown up would ease some of his guilt and allow him to heal. The town was a lot quieter; and although he couldn't disappear, he could keep those he loved from really seeing.

"The coffee shop is in that direction," Michael said, turning Noah around by the shoulders, "toward Lana's bookstore."

Noah shrugged and began to walk in the direction Michael indicated. Michael fell wordlessly in step beside him, dressed in a similar fashion to him. Boots, jeans, warm button-down shirt, and a thick coat warded off the chill. The cold morning air whistled lightly over Noah's face. He squinted against the cheerful sunlight bouncing off the bright snow, reminding him that he'd forgotten his sunglasses, too. The air was fresh and smelled faintly of pine needles, salt, and baked goods. He settled his hands more firmly inside his coat's pockets. Why had he forgotten his gloves again this morning?

"How are you?" Michael asked quietly, sensing his internal distress.

"Wondering why people think that vitamin D is the key to happiness," Noah replied sardonically.

Michael nodded and didn't pry further. He understood the pain Noah suffered; it was one of the things they shared. Both had a military background and had seen the good and the bad of a life of service. Michael was the only one of the brothers who didn't treat Noah like an injured animal. The others didn't know what to do with him, much the same as they had when Michael had returned. It was one of the main reasons Noah had relocated to Snowy Springs and not Denver when he'd left the army base. Maybe he could find what Michael had in this place.

Since Michael's return to Snowy Springs, he'd fought his own memories and yet seemed to flourish despite them. A year ago, he'd reconnected with his long-time love, Sarah Bakker; and if Noah's suspicions were correct, they would set a date for their wedding before the Christmas season was over. Noah was happy for his brother—truly happy, although those feelings did come with the sting and memory of his own loss. It was selfish to think of things that way; but at the same time, it made his loss more bearable. Michael had found his happily ever after; Noah only hoped to find peace.

"I bumped into Aaron at Sarah's last night. He said Buck's Christmas Tree Farm is hiring," Michael said as the coffee shop came into view. Snow Town Coffee was a Snowy Springs institution, or so Noah had heard. When the exodus of some of the Thomas family members had happened some years ago, the shop had not been a part of the town attractions. Time hadn't stopped in Snowy Springs.

"I suppose you want me to check it out."

Michael nodded, wearing an expression that looked something like *duh*. Noah sighed. Another thing had changed in his life. When he'd enlisted, he'd wanted to retire military. The thought of some other career had never crossed his mind until the day he'd woken up in the hospital to the news that he was an amputee and could not return to active service. Receiving the news that same day that he was a widower had shaken him to his core.

"Hey," Michael said stopping him outside the coffee shop, "I know this isn't the life you saw for yourself. I know it wasn't the one I envisioned for me. Now, I wouldn't change it for anything."

Noah was slow to nod. "Sure, I'll drive by later. Let's hope Buck is in a giving mood. You know small town gossip." He gestured down to his pant-covered prosthetic limb.

"You never know. Christmas is around the corner; and everyone's in a giving mood, even the town's busybodies," Michael said cheerfully.

Noah wanted to smack him. Michael had come back from the desert reclusive, defensive, and on edge, riddled with PTSD and regrets. Life for him had been hard. Noah rubbed the back of his neck. A lot had changed in twelve months; it certainly had for him. Nowadays, Michael was joyful, almost the same kind of man he had been growing up, just a more mature version of him. Michael said his faith had freed him from the nightmare of his captivity. Noah couldn't find any other believable explanation for the change and was inclined to believe it. God hadn't featured in Noah's life for a long time and likely never would again.

Following Michael into the entrance of Snow Town Coffee, Noah inhaled the smell of cinnamon, candy cane, and gingerbread, relieved that the smell of coffee didn't send his memories spiraling again. Red, green, and white Christmas lights blinked in succession to the tune of "Santa Claus Is Coming to Town," over the din of voices filling the air. Every store in Snowy Springs began their Christmas preparations early, and Snow Town Coffee was no exception. When the thick snow came in at the end of November, the Christmas activities were well underway and ready for the white deluge.

This year was no different. It was less than four weeks to Christmas; and already, the sidewalks and roadsides were piled high with white embankments. A small distance lay between the lights strung amid lampposts down the main street, which was lined with twinkling stars and flashing Christmas trees on long, black posts.

"I'll have two medium coffees, one with cream, one black, please, Tara," Michael said to the young woman behind the counter. She typed rapidly across the elevated keyboard.

Noah cleared his throat, glaring balefully at this brother. Michael glanced at him. "What, like you were going to order something else?"

His brother knew him too well. "I might have; that Chai tea latte looks like a good option."

"Really?" Michael raised is eyebrow. "Tara, would you please—"

Another glare from Noah cut off Michael's words. Michael coughed a laugh and turned back to the counter.

"Never mind. Just the two coffees and two peppermint-dipped doughnuts." He shrugged innocently, still sporting a huge smile.

A rough and broken chuckle shoved itself past Noah's lips in amusement.

"Order up," Tara called from the counter a few minutes later.

Michael collected the coffees and gestured to the two doughnuts beside it. "Try one. You won't regret it."

"I don't know. I'm already regretting agreeing to seeing you this morning."

Frigid air greeted them as they walked outside. Noah took a swallow of his coffee, sighing as the warmth permeated down his chest. He decided to try the doughnut, despite his dislike for red food, and smiled. It was delicious—gooey and tasty in perfect contrast to the bitter black coffee.

"It's good to see you smile," Michael said.

Noah didn't know what to do with his words. His brokenness was not a secret; and he was sure his pain bled from every thought, word, and action he took. What he hadn't known was how noticeable it was to his family, and the knowledge gave him pause. "Sorry."

"Don't be. It does get better," Michael said. "In time, it does get better."

Had those words come from anyone else, Noah would have ignored them. But Michael knew what he was talking about. He'd lived it. Noah swallowed hard against the mix of guilt, sorrow, and anger bubbling like an open wound in his chest. Could it be that easy? Time. Time would heal his gaping wounds. Time would evaporate the stone of guilt in his chest, and time would heal the torn pieces of his heart.

Chapter Two

"Megan, the doctor says it doesn't look good."

"Oh, Mia, I am so sorry."

Quiet sobs filled the line, followed by a soft clearing of a throat. "Doc's here. I'll call you later."

Megan Davis ended the phone call with her sister-in-law, her words echoing around the silent room. She scrubbed an errant tear from her cheek and tried, without success, to calm the wriggling infant in her arms. Babies picked up on tension, and Megan was sure Isaiah could feel it bleeding from her. A heaviness expanded from her core, pressing into her chest like the weight of the world. Blinking against her fatigue, her gaze swept over the glowing watch on her wrist: 2:00 a.m. More tears threatened, and she swallowed them away. Isaiah needed her to hold it together, at least until his parents returned. Crooning softly, she cuddled him closer and rubbed his back.

"Don't worry, buddy, it's all going to be okay."

It wasn't a truth; but maybe if she could convince herself of it, her body would get the message and calm her reeling emotions. It seemed to work because Isaiah snuggled closer, his little eyelids heavy with sleep, his mouth moving in a sucking motion. He wasn't hungry for his last bottle laying on the coffee table beside her, only in need of comfort. Megan retrieved the pacifier from behind her back, brushing it gently against Isaiah lips until he took it. His body became heavy against her as he slipped into sleep. *Success*, she thought as her body slumped back into her sofa.

How did she always find herself in these situations? She had a paper due in less than five hours and had hoped to spend the night editing her latest draft before submitting it. Caring for Isaiah hadn't been in her planning; but then again, neither had a life-threatening cancer diagnosis.

"I wouldn't ask unless it was an emergency," Mia, her sister-in-law, had said roughly five hours before when she and Megan's brother Tyreke had raced to the hospital. By all standards, Mia was a great sister-in-law; and Megan loved her nephew. But the timing could not have been worse. The discovery of Mr. Ambrose's cancer a few days ago had sent the entire family into a tailspin and led to Megan's current dilemma. Mia, Tyreke, and Mrs. Ambrose were all either at the hospital or at home getting some much-needed rest.

In the morning—or in a few hours, rather—they would know just how dire the news truly was and what treatment would follow. She knew her efforts to support the family were appreciated; she just wished she didn't have such an important paper due. Yawning, she stood and carried Isaiah back to the pack-and-play set up at the corner of her bedroom. It was simple, meant for one occupant. The purple duvet was strewn across her double bed, hanging off the one side, covering her laptop. A small walk-in closet was in the right corner with just enough space beside it for the bookshelf that housed her textbooks.

Her foot connected with a pair of white sneakers as she crossed the room. She stumbled over them, clutching Isaiah to her chest, careful not to wake him. It was a simple enough task to lower him to the mattress, drape a soft, fluffy blanket over him, and leave him to his sleep. The blue and white checkered blanket was comforting and desperately needed on a night like this one. Sleep was a lost cause, with her paper still unsubmitted and the hours counting down.

A short trip down the hallway brought her back to her living room. It was an open plan; one side held a flat-screen television and a hand-me-down sofa on the other side of a compact kitchen. She flipped the light switch on as she made her way to the coffee machine. Maybe some caffeine would help her sleep-deprived brain focus. On second thought, maybe a best course of action would be to get a few hours of sleep and tackle the assignment when she at least could see straight.

After some deliberation, option two won; and Megan walked back to her room. Moments later, she had covers pulled to her ears as she allowed sleep to pull her under, hoping that she would wake with enough time for her assignment.

Hours later, Megan was ripped from her sleep. Her heart raced, and she blinked rapidly. Was Isaiah all right? What time was it? She pushed back the covers and tapped her watch: 5:00 a.m. Her paper was due in four hours.

Just then, the memory caught up with her; and she glanced toward the pack-and-play. Isaiah slept soundly, his small fist curled beside his head, chest rising and falling evenly in sleep. Megan sighed as tenderness overwhelmed her before reality crashed over her again.

Pulling on her a sweater and track pants, she tip-toed out the room in search of coffee. Perhaps if Isaiah continued to sleep soundly, she would have her paper finished before he awoke. Her brain fuzzy from sleep, Megan flipped on the coffee machine, deciding on a shower to wake her as it brewed.

Less than ten minutes later, she was in the kitchen savoring the smell of freshly brewed coffee. She poured herself a cup—black, like her current state of mind—and turned on her computer. It came quickly to life, and she settled in to begin working on her final read-through of her assignment, silently praying that she would somehow have it done on time.

Two hours later, the musings of Plato, Socrates, and Friedrich Nietzsche were interrupted by a small but insistent cry coming from Megan's room. Sighing, she saved her yet-to-be-finished work and shut down the computer. Coffee cup in hand, she hurried to her bedroom and the waiting infant. It was times like these that she wished her parents were still alive.

Wow, Megan, selfish much?

It wasn't that she didn't want to help, but her final paper was important to the completion of her psychology degree and the culmination of four years of hard work. Sighing, she pushed away her arguments. Here she was whining about how unfair her life was when Mr. and Mrs. Ambrose had so much more to contend with.

Heart heavy, Megan set her coffee cup down, lifted Isaiah to her shoulder, and walked back to the kitchen, checking the clock as she passed. Mia had said she would be back by 8:00 a.m. to collect him.

One hour was better than nothing. And it seemed that one hour was all she would have.

"Did you sleep well, buddy?" she crooned to her nephew.

Isaiah cooed softly and nudged her chin with his mouth sucking impatiently.

Megan laughed. "I guess you're hungry, huh?"

Isaiah continued to suck her chin, seeming to encourage her to get on with finding him his food.

"Let's go see what your mama packed you for breakfast," Megan said, lifting the gray and white baby bag on the kitchen counter and digging into its depths for Isaiah's bottle and container of formula. Isaiah babbled happily as she placed him in the baby chair and strapped him in. Filling the bottle with warm water, she added a scoop of formula and shook it well before handing it to the baby. He latched onto the bottle, drinking with unbridled enthusiasm. Small, brown hands gripped the bottle like a lifeline.

Megan found herself chuckling at his antics. How simple life was when all you had to worry about was where your next bottle of milk was coming from. She picked him up from his high chair and nestled him in the crook of her arm while he feasted on his breakfast. Infant in one arm, she returned to small table she had in her living room and opened the laptop to return to work. The pages of her assignment waited for her to settle in and make sure the facts and figures she'd spent hours researching were correct and well-referenced.

"Death is not the worst that can happen to men–Plato." She'd read the quote many times before deciding to add it to her paper; however, after the last few days, it struck her anew. Death was something awful, an end, a taking away of a person—not just the person themselves but also all their future hopes and dreams. Like her parents. Because their lives had been cut short, there was so much they would never be a part of. On the day of her graduation, there would be two empty seats where they should have been.

She looked down at Isaiah still sucking on his bottle, grief flamed anew. They would never meet Isaiah or see him grow up. A fresh wave of anguish pressed against the back of her eyes, the pain as fresh as it had been on the first day. Each time she believed her grief had eased, it roared back to life. Perhaps that was why the paper she'd written focused on grief, the human mind, and life after death. Maybe that was the reason that Plato's quote stuck with her. If death was not the end, what more was there?

She glanced again at the clock—7:30 a.m.—and less than one-and-a-half hours before her paper was due. Anxiety rippled through her body, and she swallowed back tears of self pity. Isaiah wiggled in her arms, bottle falling to the floor. Megan rubbed her tired eyes, retrieved the fallen bottle, and stuck it back into his mouth. Isaiah continued to wriggle. He probably needed to be changed.

Once that task was taken care of, Megan pressed Isaiah to her shoulder, gently rubbing his back. The computer screen blinked to black again as it waited for her. She looked at the clock. It was hopeless; she would never get her paper in on time.

If she thought about it, her late paper was not the only reason for her misery. Tiredness aside, she still mourned that grief, compacted by the news she had just received. Wet droplets slipped down her cheeks; and she swallowed hard, trying to stop them. Mr. Ambrose would be an addition to the list of people she cared about and lost. How much sadness could one person take before that sadness took all the joy from their life and replaced it with fear and anxiety? How much suffering could one human take before it became unbearable? What more was there to life? Was it a list of achievements and successes counterbalanced by a list of failures and losses?

She thought of a quote she'd read: "To live is to suffer, to survive is to find some meaning in that suffering." Was that true? What meaning could there possibly be in all her and her family's suffering?

A Bible peeked out on the tabletop from between her books. Mrs. Ambrose had given it to Megan on the day of her parents' memorial, knowing full well that Megan did not believe. However, the book was a useful reference book for her paper, and so she had kept it.

What about the verses she'd read in 2 Corinthians 4:16-18: "Therefore we do not lose heart. Though outwardly we are wasting away, yet inwardly we are being renewed day by day. For our light and momentary troubles are achieving for us an eternal glory that far outweighs them all. So we fix our eyes not on what is seen, but on what is unseen, since what is seen is temporary, but what is unseen is eternal"? What did it mean? Was the suffering in life temporary? What was beyond death? Was there more?

Megan sighed again. How she wished she could find an answer to her questions. Maybe then, she could find some hope in all of this.

Chapter Three

"It's good to see you boys," Buck Wheeler, owner and manager of Crazy Lane Farms, said as Noah and Michael walked across the snow-covered ground toward a lot of Christmas trees.

Crazy Lane Farm had been a part of Snowy Springs for as long as Noah could remember. Buck had known the Thomas family since Noah's parents had gotten married right up until the family had left town after Michael's disappearance. In his freshman year of high school, Noah had worked through December break and the following summer at Buck's farm. The irony was not lost on him that here he was years later seeking employment again back in Snowy Springs. The farm, although it had undergone cosmetic changes over the years, still looked the same. He took it as a good sign. Perhaps it was nostalgia, or perhaps he just wanted something in his life to go right.

Pasting on a fake smile, he followed Michael over the uneven ground, doing his best to stay on his feet and not topple over. It was unsurprising that Michael walked back straight, eyes scanning the surrounding forest. As much progress as Michael had made in the last year, he would carry his years of captivity with him for the rest of his life. Noah knew those years still haunted his brother. Noah was not the only one who didn't sleep well at night, though the dreams came less often since Michael had reconnected with Sarah. Noah was grateful for the change. Knowing this, he wondered what it would take to make his own haunted dreams to disappear. A woman? He doubted it.

"Thank you, sir," Noah said.

He stepped forward to grasp Buck's outstretched hand and shook it. Michael did the same.

Being here took him back. The farm smelled like trees, earth, and snow. Rows of Christmas trees each at its own stage of growth reminded him of a simpler life where death and conflict had not reached. A pang went through his leg, prompting him back to the present where life went on and he had changed with it.

They passed the first lot of trees and went onto the hilly second. The strain of his muscles reminding him of just how much of his life was different. The adjustment to life as an amputee was difficult. At first, it was the shock of his accident, the grief over his loss, and the realization that life would never be the same. In one night, his entire future had come crashing down. Noah centered his thoughts on the present, determined to keep them on the here and now. If he let his mind wander too far, he'd either sink himself into another black mood or fall on his face.

The baling barn came into view, and Noah sighed as he remembered. Life had been so much easier then when all he'd had to worry about was which girl he wanted to ask to the spring dance and playing football. It was a long time ago, he reminded himself.

"Did you boys come to collect the tree for the community center?" Buck asked.

A twelve-foot Colorado blue spruce was the standard tree used in the Snowy Springs festivities.

"I did," Michael replied. "Sarah said to check that it was perfect." His face softened as he spoke of his fiancée.

Buck smiled. "Just like a woman, always wanting to make sure." He laughed along with Michael.

Noah's coffee churned sourly in his stomach. It was hard to bear witness to the other men's happiness while knowing he had lost his own. It rankled him that it bugged him, but there it was. He supposed he should stop mulling himself into a bad mood and get to the reason he was really at the farm.

He cleared his throat to get Buck's attention. "You posted for hands for the Christmas season in the paper? I'm here to apply."

Buck nodded slowly, eyeing Noah up and down. "You looking for work? I thought you were army for life?"

"Things change." He shrugged. "I am looking for whatever work I can find."

The severity of the accident had taken many things from him: his strength, dexterity, agility, and leg. He didn't know yet how much physical labor he was able to do with his amputation, but he would not let that stop him from finding out.

"It's physical work requiring a lot of muscle. Are you sure you are up to it?" Buck asked.

"I would love if you would give me a chance," Noah said nonchalantly.

Employing him was a gamble for Buck, and he could understand Buck's hesitancy. Christmas time was a very busy season on the tree farm, and Buck needed everyone to be able to carry their share. Although Noah's physical therapist said he was doing well and he felt better, there was no guarantee that he was able to perform the back-breaking work so soon after his crash. But the thought of sitting on his butt for one more month would drive him crazy.

Buck considered Noah for a long time, long enough that Noah was sure he would say no—not because Noah was not able but because small towns held few secrets, and what had happened the night of his accident was well known. Even if his behavior was exemplary all the years before that night, one incident had the power to destroy a solid reputation.

"Come on, Buck," Michael said. "I know you need the help after the other boys left you in the lurch a month ago."

Buck barked a loud laugh. "You got me there, son," he said. Turning to Noah, he gave him another long look. "Your head straight?"

"As an arrow, Buck. I don't know what you heard—"

A wave of Buck's hand cut Noah off mid-sentence. "I've known your family since you two were still in diapers. We've all done crazy things at the spur of the moment. One incident doesn't make a habit."

And there was the grace of a small town. While gossip spread faster than fire, people had long memories. Fear's tight grip on his chest eased; and Noah hungrily drew in a deep cleansing breath, silently thanking Whomever was out there for Buck. He found he was unable to put into thought or word the gratitude he felt for Buck. Since the accident, Noah had carried his mistake believing that he was no good to anyone; this small gesture meant more than Buck could possibly have imagined.

"Thank you," he said quietly, choking out the words. "I won't let you down,"

Buck accepted Noah's outstretched hand, clasping it in his warm, calloused one. "See that you don't."

A minute of silence passed before Buck pulled his Stetson more firmly onto his head, sliding on a pair of work-roughed gloves.

"Let's go see about that tree for the community center," Buck said, turning to stride toward the shed where the chainsaws were kept.

Noah followed, sinking his cold hands into the warm lining of his pockets, Michael close at his heels. The beauty of the simple farm became new to him as he looked around. One act of kindness had changed his day for the better, and he would not forget it. Maybe it was time to stop living in the past.

Chainsaw in hand, Buck led them over to another larger barn closer to the second driveway of the farm. "Here is where we keep the trees that are ready for baling. Bill and Jim cover the cultivations side of things. Those two louts Larry and Spence were supposed to help with digging new holes for the new saplings, baling the trees that are ready to be sold, along with whatever other duties needed to be done around the farm." Buck turned to Noah gesturing him forward. "Do you think you can handle all that?"

Noah nodded turning again to peruse the trees. From memory, he could identify a few—particularly the Fraser fir, Douglas fir, and white pine. The rest were a mystery to him; he would have to re-educate himself on the types of trees. "No problem. When would you like me to start?"

"Tomorrow, 8:00 a.m," Buck said.

"Sure."

"Good, one less thing I have to worry about. Now about that tree." Buck walked over to another group of trees and pointed to the largest one. "Do you think this one would be suitable—or, in Sarah's words, 'perfect'?"

Michael circled the tree twice, shrugged, and turned to Noah. "What do you think?"

"Looks fine," he said.

Thirty minutes later, the tree was chopped down, sanitized, and baled, ready for transportation to the community center. It cheered Noah considerably to realize that he had held onto the skills he'd learned while in high school, most of them coming from muscle memory.

They said their goodbyes to Buck, loaded up the tree, and were on their way back to town before long.

"That turned out better than I thought," Michael said.

"That makes two of us," Noah said.

He was going to kill Michael. When Noah had agreed to help transport the annual Christmas tree to the community center, he had not counted on being puked on by his nephew, Brady. He sniffed. The smell of sour milk burned his nose, and he did his best not to gag in response to the nauseating aroma.

"I am so sorry," Susie said, handing him an antiseptic wet wipe. "I think he's had enough ice cream for one day."

Susie, his brother Ben's wife, continued to hand him wipe after wipe until the huge splotch of throw up was wiped clean from his shirt. It did little to take the smell from his nose; each time he breathed, he could smell the offensive odor again.

"It's not so bad," he said, smiling gently at a harassed-looking Susie. "I should have been more careful with the little guy." Tossing his nephew several times in the air with a belly full of ice cream was not his finest moment. Next time, he would be more careful.

Ben nodded in sympathy, "One thing I've learned in my very short time as a parent is always expect the unexpected; that way, you are never surprised."

Noah rolled his eyes as Michael tsked. Brady reached for Noah; and despite the rank smell on his shirt, he didn't have the heart to say no. Taking the small boy into his arms again, he continued his exploratory journey around the community center. Each doorway held a different activity; and Noah was glad that Michael and Aaron had been able to salvage the fair last year when the roof caved in, so the traditions from his childhood could be continued. He'd been genuinely surprised at the rush of pleasure he'd felt when he walked into the community center with the Christmas tree on his shoulder and seen the bustling stalls just the way he remembered. It was comforting and a window into a world that was still pure and innocent, untainted by life—where anything was possible and joy was as simple as making a garland or drinking peppermint hot chocolate. He'd inhaled the scents of gingerbread, chestnuts, and pine needles as he was guided to the stage where the tree would rest for the remainder of the season.

Brady pulled at his arm, swinging his little fist in front of Noah's face. "Where do you want to go next?"

"I think he wants to see the dancing elves show," Susie said, pointing to a doorway bordered with white and red tinsel. Loud, jovial Christmas music belted from the room, in time with the flashing white and red Christmas lights. Huge, glittering baubles hung at the four corners of the doorway.

"In there," he said.

Brady nodded and babbled something Noah couldn't understand.

"Okay, bud, lets see what's happening with the elves."

Chapter Four

"Thank you so much. I'm so sorry that took us so long. My father..." Mia reached eagerly for the baby in Megan's arms, cuddling the little wriggling form close to her chest.

Tyreke entered behind his wife, taking Megan into his arms and hugging her. "Thanks," he said before releasing her. "Amana phoned at 4:00 a.m., and there wasn't anyone else we could take him to."

"It was a pleasure to spend time with him," she said, hoping the strain of the past hours didn't sink into her words.

She hadn't told Mia and Tyreke of her pending paper, nor the fact that it now would be more than a day late. They had far more important things to worry about than a due date that had been set months in advance. Megan would speak to her faculty advisor and explain, hoping that he would still accept the paper in time to allow her to graduate. The credit was already a semester late, delayed by the death of her parents. For months, she'd been unable to do much more than wake up, and her grief had set her academic schedule into a tailspin and pushed back her graduation date. History seemed to be repeating itself.

She shook her head, determined once again to finish her degree this semester before moving forward to her master's program. If she managed to convince Professor Wallace to accept the late assignment, she amended.

Suppressing another sigh, she placed a goodbye kiss on Isaiah's fuzzy head, breathing in his lovely baby smell while Mia fussed with the baby and Tyreke circled Megan's apartment packing up Isaiah's things. He left the pack-and-play assembled in the corner of her room, and Megan supposed it was for the best. Who knew what the next weeks and months held for the family?

"Thank you again," Mia said. "It means a lot to us to have your help and support."

Megan waved away Mia's words. "It all good. Always happy to help. Take care and let me know as soon as you have any other information."

She ushered the family of three out the door and into the bright light of her apartment hallway. She closed the door behind them, leaning against it and resting her tired eyes for a moment before using the sturdy door to push herself upright. She wandered around the apartment considering what to do next—sleep or face the firing squad? Sleep wouldn't happen, not with that over her head. The firing squad it was. Facing her professor couldn't wait any longer.

Circling around the apartment, she collected her books, piling them neatly on the table. She found her laptop, slipped it into the cover, and then put both into her messenger bag, along with her purse, phone, and an extra set of research notes just in the case she had to defend her position. There was no doubt in her mind that Professor Wallace would be less than impressed with her tardy assignment, but maybe he would have some grace when he heard the reason it was late. Her morning workout, however, could not wait. One more hour would not make any difference to the already late paper.

Thirty minutes later, refreshed and ready to face the world, Megan locked the apartment door behind her and carefully stepped from the lobby of her apartment building. Slush and snow covered the icy sidewalk, and she didn't fancy the idea of landing on her butt because she was in too much of hurry today. Ice and snow crunched under her boots as she walked over the wet concrete. A gust of freezing cold whipped over her; and she shivered, drawing the neck of her winter coat tighter around her face. The sun shone weakly in the sky, and plumes of grayish brown snow clouds gathered on the horizon portending snow later. Their covering made the hour seem later than it was.

Her forward movement came to an abrupt halt as she came to her car. A wave of panic skittered through her chest. She blinked and blinked again. No, this could not be happening. But it was. The front tire of her red hatchback was as flat as a squished piece of pizza sunk into the mound of snow collected by the morning snowmobiles.

"What?" She gasped.

Not only was she standing on the edge of being unable to graduate; but because of her tire trouble, she would also be incapable of attending the meeting with her professor and unable to explain the tardiness of her paper. She glanced down at her phone: 8:00 am. Maybe if she hurried, she would still be able to make the meeting, albeit a few minutes late.

Grumbling under her breath, she popped the trunk of her car and hauled the spare tire onto the drenched road. It landed with a splash, spraying freezing drops of wet ice onto her black leggings. Great, one more thing to go wrong this morning. Next, she dug around for the jack and spanner. Tyreke had made sure she had these in a place that was easily accessible for use.

"Can I help you with that tire?" a voice asked from behind her. It was warm and clear with a husky edge to it.

Megan turned toward the voice, coming face to face with a set of ocean blue eyes that crinkled at the edges. Her gaze lifted higher. Taller than her by at least half a foot, the man had rich, dark brown hair and a rugged, handsome face. His face was darkly tanned, despite the cold weather, like he had spent too much time out in the sun. The blue denim, sheep skin-lined jacket accentuated the broadness of his shoulders, and the narrowness of his jean covered hips and long legs. Unsurprisingly, he wore work boots. A gentle smile curved his mouth, growing larger the longer she stared at him. An eyebrow raised in question and snapped her back to reality. She still hadn't answered him, and she was still staring.

Clearing her throat, Megan regathered her thoughts. "Sh-sure," she said, stumbling back against the trunk of her car, knees weak.

Megan had never believed in attraction at first sight and feeling loopy over a man until this very moment. It had always been silly to her the way women swooned over handsome men. Clearly, those women were onto something if they had ever met *this* man. Another man just as handsome as the first, his coloring and eyes confirming he was close family, stepped up beside the first man. He looked to be the younger of the two. His smile was more open and less . . . pensive?

"Do you have a jack?" he asked, bending over her trunk.

Megan nodded, gesturing to the middle. "Inside, I think. There is a wrench, I assume, in there, too."

The younger man nodded and got to work retrieving the wrench and jack from inside her trunk.

"Noah Thomas," the first man said, holding out his hand in greeting. "This is my brother Michael."

"Megan Davis," she replied. "Nice to meet you both. Thank you for stopping by to help."

"We've met before," Michael said, fitting the jack to the underside of her car while his brother fitted the wrench and began to lift the car. "At the bookstore—my fiancée, Sarah, and her mother, Lana, run it."

Thoughts scrambled her brain, and then she remembered. When Megan had moved to Snowy Springs, she'd searched for a bookstore that held a particular textbook she needed for her philosophy class. Sarah managed to find the book and sell it to Megan at a great price. "That's right. Sarah is a whizz with finding out-of-print books."

Michael smiled proudly. "She is something, isn't she?"

Noah choked back a laugh and was playfully swatted by his brother. Their interaction reminded Megan of how things were between her and Tyreke before everything in their life had fallen apart. They were still close; however, Tyreke had his own family to worry about nowadays, and Megan felt more and more like she was being left behind.

The two men worked in tandem loosening the nuts and removing the tire from her car. Just then, the tire slipped from Michael's hands, careening into Noah's leg and forcing him backward at an awkward angle into the nearby bench. The bottom half of Noah's leg separated from his body, sliding in the opposite direction of where he landed with a painful grunt on the hard concrete.

"Noah," Michael shouted, grabbing the tire in one hand before it rolled into the road and hauling it with him toward his brother. He reached with his other hand for the leg, bringing it within reach of Noah's hands.

Megan stared dazed at the two before taking a shaky step forward and kneeling beside the two men.

"Are you okay?" she asked Noah, bewildered by what had just taken place. Was it a dumb question to ask even if she really wanted to know?

The face that had been so open and friendly moments before glowered at her, his color high and angry. His eyes blazed with intense emotions. Unconsciously, she moved backward, then took a deep breath and held her ground.

"I'm fine," he muttered, snatching the leg from Michael, his tone harsh and ashamed. He looked down. The muscles of his jaw were working so that she could see them flex and bulge. "I said I'm fine. You can go now."

Michael met her gaze, a silent apology written over his face.

She nodded and rose to her feet, moving back to stand by her car.

"Here, can you hold this?" Michael asked, pointing to the tire. "I need to help him up."

Wrenched out of her confusion, Megan nodded, unable to look away as Michael lifted his brother to stand and helped him hobble to the bench. Noah sat down, not looking at her as he reattached a prosthetic leg to his lower limb, tugging his pants leg over it as soon as he was done. He stared down at the ground, his jaw still working as if chewing rocks.

Michael sighed, looked at his brother for a long time, and walked back over to Megan. "Let's get this finished, and you can be on your way."

Dumbfounded, all Megan could do was nod.

It didn't take Michael long to refit the spare tire onto the front axle, tighten the nuts, and place the ruined tire back into her trunk with everything else.

"There," he said, "all set. If you need to find a mechanic to replace that tire, I can give you a number."

She nodded. She should have just thanked him and let the day go on, but there was something about the way Noah folded into himself that sent a spasm of compassion through her.

"Is he going to be okay?" she whispered to Michael, hoping Noah wouldn't overhear them.

Michael glanced over his shoulder at his brother, concern bending his brow. "In time."

There was something about the way he said the words that made Megan think that he knew what he was talking about like he had walked a journey, too. Hadn't everyone? A tightness rose in her chest, awakening a feeling of kinship with the man.

"Thank you both for your help. I really appreciate it," she said. She looked at Noah again, trying to catch his gaze. Her efforts were met with little success; he didn't lift his head but just stared down at the pavement. Questions popped into her mind—not a mere curiosity but something else. She pushed away the feeling; she was most likely late already for her meeting and couldn't afford anymore delays.

With one last glance at the two brothers, she climbed into her car, waved, and pulled out into the morning traffic. Her thoughts still focused on the man sitting on a street bench, pain coming off him in waves, and wondered if she would ever see him again.

Chapter Five

He didn't know which had taken the worst hit, his pride or his leg. Grappling with the fittings of his prosthetic limb, Noah reattached the mechanism before rolling down the leg of his jeans. The seat of his pants was wet from the puddle he had fallen into. Shame burned his skin, making his face hot. The familiar depression sucked him in like a black hole. Useless. He couldn't even change a tire without completely humiliating himself.

He sighed, cursing under his breath. The feeling of inadequacy scorched his chest, merging with his shame until his whole body felt like it was on fire. Anger quickly joined the feeling; and he strained against its tide, flexing and releasing the muscles of his hands. He inhaled deeply, wrestling against the darkness, pushing it back but only by a short measure. *Snap out of it, Noah.*

A cold wind blew, cooling some of his humiliation; and he lifted his head, studying his brother as Michael worked on a particularly stubborn nut. The woman crossed his view again, and he found his gaze lingering on her. Megan Davis, of medium build and slender, had clear skin a warm ochre that matched perfectly to her hair, which was a mass of mahogany curls. It bounced around her face as she moved. But it was her eyes that held him the first time they had lifted to meet his—brown, like the color of warm oak and bearing a lingering wealth of emotion that spoke to his own. He should stop watching her; and yet he continued to stare as she pulled a rubber band from her wrist and secured the mass of curls at the nape of her neck, noting the graceful way she moved, the gentle sway of her hips and . . .

He blinked hard, squeezing his eyelids together. What was going on with him? He squeezed the bridge of nose and then trailed his hand over his head, mussing his already-disarrayed hair. Groaning softly, he pulled on his woolen hat and leaned back into the bench, waiting—stewing in his self-pity, if he was honest with himself. Thinking about any woman was a bad idea, no matter the fact that Megan Davis was the first woman he had looked at twice since losing his wife.

"There. All done," Michael said, resting back on his heels before rising.

Megan leaned closer to Michael and said something too low for Noah to hear. Michael glanced over his shoulder and then said something back just as low. Megan's gaze met his again, and he could see compassion shining there.

"Thank you," she said.

He nodded, turning his gaze once again to the floor. The warmth of her thank you quickly disappeared, and cold lingered in his chest once more.

"You're welcome, Megan. Do you live close by?" Michael asked.

Amused, Noah glanced up at his brother, wryly thinking how good Sarah was for his usually sullen brother.

"Yes, Crystal Apartments just over there." She shoved her hands deeper into the pockets of her red puffer jacket, coupled with black leggings and ankle-high black boots. Despite all his reservations, he was noticing her again. He quietly cleared his throat, hoping that Michael would take the hint and give them a reason to leave. Michael didn't take the hint.

"We're meeting Sarah at Snow Town Coffee. Would you like to join us?" Michael said.

His body stilled with shock. What was Michael doing? "Great," he muttered under his breath; and yet he looked at Megan, waiting for her answer and was oddly bereft by it.

Megan shook her head. "No, thank you, I'm on my way to the university to sort an issue with my professor. Please tell Sarah I say hi."

"Sure, maybe next time. Maybe see you Sunday?"

"Maybe," Megan said.

There was real regret in her tone as if she wanted to say yes, and yet something was holding her back. He knew a lot of people didn't believe in God. Did Megan? He'd grown up in a God-fearing household, often wondering why people didn't believe. *What about you?* It was fair to say he knew of God, had known God; but he and God had parted ways a long time ago. And who was he to judge knowing this about himself?

His attention was drawn back to their conversation when Megan turned and headed toward her car. She slid into the driver's seat, lifted her hand in a wave, and merged with the slow-moving traffic. Snowy Springs was not a large town, but he doubted he would run into her again. And that was good thing, he reminded himself.

"You okay?" Michael asked, taking a seat beside him. Noah nodded solemnly, trying to shove his thoughts away from Megan.

"Yeah, fine, just this . . . " He waved his hand above his leg, the familiar surge of anger filling his chest. Why did he go out that night? What had possessed him to get behind the wheel of a car with a healthy dose of rage and one of the deadliest thunderstorms Colorado had ever seen raging? He rubbed his hand down his face, then clenched his hands together in his lap. "Sarah's waiting," he said quietly.

Michael nodded and rose from the bench. Noah followed.

"Pretty girl," Michael said.

"Shut it," Noah said, ignoring Michael's chuckle.

Snow Town Coffee was a five-minute walk. Noah cautiously navigated the sidewalk, carefully avoiding any puddles of ice until, at last, the coffee shop came into view. It was a quaint place, large exterior windows decorated with the season's finery framed with dark wooden borders. An antique wooden door stood as the entrance. The friendly tingle of silvers bells welcomed them as they entered. It was blessedly warm inside after the cold, and the aroma of coffee filled the air.

Noah shucked his coat from his shoulders. His sullen mood grew darker witnessing Michael and Sarah smiling happily at each other. So much in love. Had he and Teneal ever looked like that? Probably, at some point early on in their relationship. *Not today, please not today.* He didn't want to dwell on the past any longer, nor ruin his brother's time with his fiancée. Maybe he should just get his coffee to go and leave the two to their planning. He wasn't good company, not in this black mood.

He turned to leave. Michael gently grabbed his shoulder, steering him toward Sarah, Juliette, and Lana seated in a booth beside a rectangular window outlined with bright white Christmas lights. The sounds of "Santa Claus Is Coming to Town" played just above the din of coffee shop customers. Servers moved and bobbed to the music as they circled tables, delivered orders, and seated customers.

"Just say hi and then you can go. I know you're eager to get to the Christmas tree farm this morning," Michael said as he seated himself beside Sarah and kissed her quickly.

Lana beamed with pride, and Noah couldn't help but be happy for his brother. After everything, Michael had found his home. Had Teneal been home for him? He'd thought so; she had been everything he'd wanted in a woman with a head of wild red hair, seductive curves, and a voice that could make his toes curl. When they'd been out, she'd drawn everyone's attention like bees to honey—just the right amount of friendly and, by far, to his reckoning, the sexiest woman in the room. Just thinking about their first months of marriage made his blood run hot.

He cleared his throat, quietly reminding himself of how the marriage had ended. That cooled him. His thoughts drifted to the moment he'd walked into their empty apartment, back from a lengthy deployment, assuming everything would be just the same as when he had left. He'd been wrong. So very disastrously wrong. And then he'd found the note . . .

"Black," he said, his attention diverted from himself by Michael's shove to his shoulder. "To go, please."

"Right away," the young woman said, turning to the rest of the table, quickly taking their orders.

"What puts you in such a pleasant mood this morning, Noah?" Lana asked.

Michael snorted, and Sarah covered her mouth to hide a smile.

Noah drew a deep breath in through his nose. "What? My mood's fine. Just wonderful," he finished sarcastically.

"Don't you sass me, boy," Lana said. There was no heat in her words, just compassion and a motherly worry.

"I'm fine," Noah repeated and was grateful that Lana let the subject drop.

If only Michael had taken the same cue. "I think Noah's just trying to stick his eyes back in his head. They nearly fell out earlier."

Noah shot a glare at his brother.

"Do tell," Sarah said.

"Do you remember Megan Davis? From the bookstore a few weeks ago?"

"Yes, she was looking for a textbook for university. What does she have to do with Noah's eyes?"

A wide smile slid over his brother's face, and Noah seriously considered slapping his hand over Michael's mouth to shush him.

"Nothing," he said gruffly.

Thankfully, a steaming cup of black coffee in a cardboard take-away cup was placed on the table in front of him. He didn't wait to say thank you; he picked up the cup, nodded to Michael and the rest of the tables occupants, and headed out the door.

It was a good thing that the doctor at his appointment yesterday said he could drive himself around. He didn't have to rely on Michael anymore to get from point A to point B. The walk to where his dark green pickup was parked at the back of the building was quick and without any hazard of him falling this time. The muscles in his leg were still smarting from his earlier tumble, but he was determined that the slight pain would not stop him from going to work today. After all, Buck had shown faith in Noah; and he could do no less than try his utmost not to let Buck down.

He took a long swallow of coffee as he climbed into the cab and got the engine started, waiting a few minutes for the car to heat up; then he was on the way to Buck's farm. The farm was on the outskirts of town; and while the drive was not overly long, it was still a fair distance from where he stayed with Michael. The light covering of snow that had begun to fall in the morning was slowly getting heavier, the flakes multiplying until the tarred road became covered in a dense layer of white. The truck handled the icy drive easily, prepared and fitted for the kind of weather at this time of year.

After almost an hour, he pulled into Crazy Lane Farm, driving to a lot near the farm house and coming to a stop. Taking the empty coffee cup with him, he climbed from the cab and crunched over the snow-covered ground toward the main farmhouse to find Buck.

"Buck, you in here?" he called, pushing open the wooden entrance door further.

"In the study," Buck said.

Noah shucked his coat, took off his boots, and walked across the wooden floor toward the study.

"Didn't expect to see you in this weather," Buck said as Noah entered the room.

"Well, you said 8:00 a.m., and here I am."

Buck nodded thoughtfully. "I'm not sure how long this snow is going to keep coming; there are a batch of trees I need chopped and baled before tomorrow for an order placed by the mayor."

"Shouldn't be a problem," Noah said. "What kind of tree does the mayor want?"

"Three Colorado blue spruce trees for the mayor's Christmas party and two Douglas firs for the elementary school's Christmas program." Buck looked him up and down. "Do you think you can manage?"

"Yup, will you stand look out for me?"

Buck nodded. "Sure. Get your things; we need to get those trees down before this snowstorm turns into a real mess."

Chapter Six

*H*ere goes nothing. Megan drew a deep breath, mentally rehearsing for the last time the spiel she would deliver to Professor Wallace in the hopes that he would reconsider her position and allow her to submit her assignment without penalties. She couldn't afford the penalties to her grades, although a penalized grade would be better than no grade at all.

Climbing from her car, she glanced down at the tire, sparing a thought for the two brothers who had helped her that morning, especially the one she couldn't stop thinking about. Taking a deep breath, she refocused her thoughts on the battle she was about to wage, leaving behind the memory of one Noah Thomas. What a confusing man. *No, focus, Megan.*

Snow crunched under her boots as she hurried across the parking lot, along the brick red pathway which was almost invisible covered by the falling snow. She relished the warmth of the building striding across the linoleum floors in search of the faculty offices. She'd only met Professor Wallace twice in her studies, once to ask him a question on a psychology assignment and the other to inform him that she would need to move her Cognitive Sciences course to another semester. Those two interactions with the professor had been pleasant; however, she was not so sure that this one would be. She could only pray that the professor was in an understanding mood.

Gathering up her courage, she pushed open the glass door and walked to the nearest desk. "I'm here to see Professor Wallace," she said to the smiling young lady.

"Down the hallway to the left."

"Thank you."

Professor Brian Wallace sat at his corner desk bent over something on his computer. He had salt and pepper hair, was in his forties or fifties, and wore the stereotypical outfit of a professor—chinos, a button-up shirt, and a tweed coat. As Megan neared his office, the professor lifted his head; seeing her, he nodded once, gestured to the seat opposite his desk, and then turned his attention back to what he was doing.

Butterflies filled her stomach, and her hands clenched around the strap of her messenger as she drew a deep breath. *It was now or never.* "Professor Wallace?" she asked.

"Ah, Miss Davis, what brings you to my office today?" He gestured for Megan to enter the office, closing the lid of his laptop as he did.

"I need an extension on my philosophy paper. I know it was due yesterday; but circumstances beyond my control happened, and I was unable to submit my paper." Direct and to the point. There was no need for idle flattery. Professor Wallace would see right through it.

"I assume there is a very good reason as to why you need the extension," he said, watching her carefully—studying her, really. She supposed in his profession, he'd probably met a lot of students whose excuses had ranged from late night parties to forgotten holidays. She hoped her track record would be enough for him to see past the excuses of her peers and see her individual need.

"Yes," she said softly, "my brother and his wife, Mia, were at the hospital with her father. They left my six-month-old nephew, Isaiah, with me. Her father has Stage Four cancer, and they aren't sure how long he will have to live." She felt a lump form in her throat as the news assaulted her afresh. She blinked hard against her roiling emotions. How were they going to go on without the steady presence of Mr. Ambrose?

"I am sorry to hear that, Megan. I am sure it was a great shock for your family." His voice was gentle and compassionate and did nothing to help her already tender emotions.

She glanced down at her entangled fingers, fighting back her tears. "Yes, it was completely unexpected."

Professor Wallace turned back to his computer and tapped a few times on the keys, then leaned back into his chair, rubbing his chin as if he were contemplating something.

"As you are a model student"—he gestured to the computer screen—"and I see you have done your best to catch up the credits that you missed in past years, I am willing to give you another week and let this extension stand without penalties. Do you think this would allow you to get your assignment in?"

Relief sweet and pure loosened the hard knot of tension in Megan's chest. She forced out a slow breath. "Thank you, and yes, I will make sure it is done."

He was quiet for a moment and then drew a decisive breath. "Could I pray for you and your family?"

What harm could it do? She wasn't a believer herself in the miracle of prayer; in this moment, however, her family could use any help they could get. "Yes, I would appreciate it."

Professor Wallace bowed his head, closing his eyes. Megan wasn't sure what to do, so she imitated his actions and closed her eyes. As his soft words flowed in the room between them, she felt as if she was being taken into a giant, warm hug. The feeling was so all-encompassing that the tears she tried so hard to hold back flowed down her cheeks, dripping onto her hands. She quickly scrubbed them away with her hand, hoping she hadn't smudged the little mascara she had applied earlier.

"Amen," Professor Wallace ended and lifted his gaze once again to her, silently handing her a few tissues from the box beside his computer.

"Thank you, Professor." She swallowed. "For everything."

"You are welcome, Ms. Davis. I will continue to pray for your family."

Without another word, she gathered her things and her composure and left the office feeling lighter and more hopeful than when she'd arrived.

It was only when she was back in her car that she realized that the trip to the university had taken her longer than usual; and if she didn't hustle, she would be horribly late for her shift at Snow Town Coffee. She flipped on her wipers to clear the coating of cotton candy-like snow from her windshield, opening her view to the other cars in the parking lot, and waited impatiently for her car to warm.

The temperature change between the warm building and the cold outside bit into her hands. She'd forgotten her gloves again. Rubbing them together vigorously before the vents, she sighed. One problem down, another to go. By the looks of things, the snow was coming down harder than before. At last, the car was warm enough to drive. She eased the accelerator pedal down. Ice-covered snow was always a danger during the winter, and it was better to be safe than sorry. The thin layer that lay on the ground from the previous night's snow was rapidly increasing in depth as the snow sheeted down in torrents hard enough that her wipers frantically whirred over her windshield, their efforts making little impact on the driving storm.

Megan turned from the lot and onto the main road, thankful for the lack of traffic. If she didn't have a job to get to, she would have parked herself in the library until the snowstorm passed. As it was, she would already be late. A call to Grace would probably be sensible. Her phone connected to handsfree as a cheerful voice rang over the sound system.

"Snow Town Coffee. Natalie speaking. How can I help you today?"

"Nat, it's Megan. Is Grace around?"

"Just a minute. Let me see if I can find her." Muted sounds came across the line as she waited for her boss to pick up. The coffee shop sounded awfully busy for this kind of weather.

"Grace here."

"Grace, its Megan. I'm afraid I am stuck in the snowstorm and running late for my shift."

Grace sighed heavily. "Yes, it's hit here, too. Everyone seems to have taken refuge in the coffee shop, and we are swamped. Please come in as soon as possible. Aurora called in sick, and I am already a server short for this shift."

"I will. Thank you, and I am sorry to leave you in lurch."

"Just get here safely as soon as possible."

"Thanks, Grace. I will." With that, she ended the call and concentrated all her attention on the increasing layers of ice drenching the road.

The university passed from sight, and she soon found herself in the country areas between the university and the town. Open stretches of trees lined each side of the road, creating a wall of white and green. Gorgeous patterns of snow formed on the mixture of blue spruce and fir trees, spreading as far as the eye could see. Once and again, a tree would stand out covered by the soft, warm glow of Christmas lights. She smiled, despite the anxiety she felt. Winter in Snowy Springs was beautiful, its colors clean and fresh.

Panic flickered in her body as her tires careened slightly to the left, drawing Megan's attention back to the snow-covered road. In some places, the black tar was no longer clearly visible, muted by the grayish layer of precipitation. She gently touched her brake pedal, slowing the momentum of her car to a crawl. Pathways cut by other cars over the black top had all but disappeared in the face of the storm. It was becoming increasingly difficult to navigate between the residual humps guiding her on the road.

Megan leaned forward, looking up at heavy brownish colored clouds that hung in the sky with no sign of disappearing anytime soon. Silence permeated the air, all sound muted by the blowing tempest covering the world in a rising layer of white.

Over the next rise, the tail of the car swerved to the right. Her heart thundered in response. Megan tightened her grip on the steering wheel, blowing out a long, soothing breath. It would be wise for her to find a place to wait out the storm, lest she find herself waiting it out in a ditch alongside the road.

She slowed the car to a crawl, tracking her gaze left and right in the hopes that somewhere in the deluge, she would find a safe place to stop. Fifteen minutes of heart-pounding tension passed before she finally sighted a large red and green sign: Crazy Lane Christmas Tree Farm. She released another heavy breath, working her neck muscles as she turned into the bumpy drive, careful to keep her car in between the previously tracked humps of snow made by another seemingly larger vehicle.

The drive was slow and long, bringing an old but well-kept farmhouse into view. The eves sparkled with white and blue lights unaffected by the clouds of white falling from the sky. Her tension eased when she saw a large, brightly lit Christmas tree out front on the wooden porch. Surely whoever lived here and had such a great Christmas tree couldn't be dangerous, right? What choice did she have? Either take a chance with the farmhouse or the snowstorm.

Another heavy sheet of snow dumped from the heavens, making her mind up for her. Option one it was. As she slowed her car to a crawl, the steering turned sluggishly, a testimony to the growing layers of snow as she turned and brought the car to a stop. The porch wasn't that far away; however, there was a thick, knee-high layer of white between her and it. Megan had no idea whether she would be able to get her car out once the storm had passed, but that was a problem for later.

Gathering her messenger bag, she climbed from the car, her strides long and high as she crossed the short distance to the front door. She knocked twice and then waited for someone to open the door.

Chapter Seven

"Just one more should do it," Buck said.

Noah braced his foot against a fir tree stump, bending low at the waist to see where his cut with the ax had landed. Noah and Buck were out in the tree lot, four trees packed onto the back of Buck's pickup, the fifth one waiting to be loaded. Snow showered down, burying the base of the fir tree he had just cleared. He set the chainsaw down beside him, rubbed his hands together, and picked it up again, activating the choke and pressing the decompression button. The chainsaw roared to life, vibrating in his hands.

"Ready?" he asked.

"Ready."

Buck braced the twelve-foot tree beside him as Noah fitted the saw to the base. A shower of wood chips littered the ground, rattling against the protection glasses over Noah's eyes.

"Get it in between the bottom branches so that there is enough space on the trunk," Buck said again for the fifth time. Noah didn't acknowledge or dismiss the information; Buck had repeated the same instruction as they'd gone from tree to tree preparing the mayor's order.

When the fir tree tipped, Noah gave it a gentle shove, guiding it down to the snow-packed ground. It landed in a cloud of white powder. Noah turned off the chainsaw.

"That's it," Buck said, tipping his head forward to remove the build up of snow on the brim of his hat.

Noah did the same, dusting the layer of snow from his own head and removing the safety glasses and placing them into his pocket.

"Let's head back; we can't do much more today."

Buck gathered the one end of the tree under his arm and waited for Noah to lift the base. Together, they secured it on the back of Buck's pickup ready to be transported.

Cold to the bone and leg aching, Noah gratefully climbed into the cab. It was probably ten below; and although he was dressed for the weather, it didn't stop the driving wind from cutting through his clothes and taking the heat from his body. He removed his gloves, throwing them onto the seat beside him while his thoughts, left alone, ran to Megan. Try as he might, he couldn't seem to get his thoughts off the woman, which was its own kind of torture. He had no business thinking of Megan; and yet here he was wondering about her again.

Buck turned over the ignition, bringing the heater to life. In a few minutes, the cab was at a pleasant temperature, the heat warming the cold muscles in Noah's body. When did he get to be such an old man, he mused silently.

"It's really coming down out there," Buck said, gearing the truck into motion.

Noah nodded and leaned his head against the rest, closing his eyes. The drive across the fields back to the farmhouse was bumpy, the mounting snow slowing their progress over the unpaved open fields until they finally came to stop beside it.

"How long do you think this storm will hang on?" Noah asked as they headed into the warm house.

Buck glanced up. "Looks like its going to carry on for a while yet. Maybe three or four hours. We might be able to bind up the mayor's order later in the afternoon."

Noah and Buck worked together to fill the fireplace with wood and kindling before lighting it. As the flame licked its way over the dry logs, the room began to thaw. Noah shucked his outer coat, warming his hands beside the open flame and adding another few logs. Buck did the same and then sat down in a brown leather easy chair, one of the three placed around the room. A square, rustic coffee table was in the middle of an understated red, navy blue, and brown circular rug. Photos and hunting memorabilia starred as décor aging the room.

"Okay, I hope we managed to get the order done," Noah replied, relishing in the warmth of the room. The last few hours at Buck's had been difficult as Noah found new ways to stand and bend to accommodate his leg.

Although the leg worked a lot the same as a flesh leg, there were some differences. Part of the process of having a prosthetic limb was learning to navigate around its use; and seeing as this was the first time Noah had really put it to the test, his muscles ached in places he hadn't before. He sighed quietly, hearing the voice of his brother again. Time—it would take time.

His dark thoughts shifted as a hesitant knock signaled someone at the front door. Noah turned toward the sound, noting that Buck had done the same.

"Were you expecting someone?"

Buck shook his head. "Maybe it one of my neighbors. Old Redford has been battling with his bull—probably got loose again. I'll go see who it is."

Noah nodded, suppressing a sigh. If it was the bull, Buck would need help. Pushing to his feet, he followed Buck to the door, stretching and massaging his aching muscles. The door opened.

"Hello," a young female voice called. "Is there anyone home?"

Noah froze. Even though he had only first heard the voice that morning, it squeezed something inside him, freeing an emotion he was very sure he did not like.

"My name is Megan Davis. I don't mean to intrude. I just need a place to wait until the storm passes." She peered around the edge of door, her expression apprehensive.

Noah stilled the riot his emotions were in and followed Buck closer to the door, forcing nonchalance by leaning against the newel post at the end of the staircase.

"Come on in, Megan. It's just two old boys here."

There she was, shifting from foot to foot as she looked around the room. Seeing him, her fearful expression cleared, softening into a smile. Was she happy to see him?

"You're welcome to wait here from the storm. I'm Buck Wheeler; the gentleman behind me is Noah Thomas." Buck reached out, taking Megan's hand in two of his. "You're cold to the bone. Come on, let's get you to the fire; so you can warm up."

"Thank you, I appreciate you letting me just stop in at your home," Megan said, glancing at him again, her relief at his presence evident.

How was he supposed to forget about her if she kept on appearing in his life at random times? He forced his body into stillness, bracing against the unwelcoming feeling she seemed to awaken in him as she passed him. The smell of her subtle perfume wafted to him, and he stopped himself from taking a long inhale. He didn't follow them; instead, he turned on his heel and headed for the kitchen. It would be much safer for his peace of mind there.

Buck's kitchen had a simple layout. Wooden cabinets formed a boxy U shape around an aged table that could seat eight or twelve people. Coffee grinds and powered creamer held a permanent position beside the percolator at the one end. Mechanically, he measured out the grinds and set the machine to brew. What was Michael up to today? he wondered, deliberately steering his thoughts from the quiet conversation in the other room—a conversation that was getting louder.

"It smells wonderful in here," Megan said, jarring him from his thoughts. Like an unwelcome intruder, she entered the kitchen, Buck close at her heels. Dressed in a pair of black leggings, a chunky knitted green sweater, and boots, she was breathtakingly beautiful. His chest pinched painfully.

"Nothing like a good cup of coffee on a cold winter's day," he said, tapping the coffee machine and feeling a bit like an idiot.

"Would be wonderful if we had some cookies," Buck chimed in as Megan nodded. "Megan, do you bake? I would, but I don't know the one end of a mixer from the other."

Megan's expression turned to surprise. "Sometimes. I'm pretty handy with a recipe."

"My wife used to bake." Buck smiled fondly. "I miss her gingerbread cookies."

A myriad of emotions crossed over Megan's face, and Noah wondered if his own flitted across his face as easily. He hoped they didn't.

Buck and Marianne had been married for as long as Noah had known him, probably even before Noah was born. She'd died this past summer of complications with a chest infection. Buck still managed to smile. Noah wondered how he did it; he hadn't been able to since Teneal had died. Maybe it was because his marriage hadn't ended happily.

"If you have a recipe, I can make some for you," Megan offered.

Compassion burned from those soft, brown eyes, and he again wondered if she knew how easily she broadcasted what she felt.

"If it's no trouble," Buck began.

"None at all. It'll be fun—a thank you for letting me stay." Megan smiled, taking the breath from Noah's lungs again.

What was the matter with him? Why did he feel like this?

Buck opened a wide drawer beside the oven, retrieving a well-loved recipe book from it. The cover was orange and yellow, the pages browned with age.

"This belonged to my wife," Buck said, handing the book to Megan. "It has everything she ever made. I think the recipe is in here somewhere." Megan laid the recipe book open in the middle of the kitchen counter, the two bending their heads closer to the black faded writing. There was something cozy about the way Megan leaned over to point out something to Buck. A feeling like . . . What was the feeling? Attraction? Compassion? Empathy? Whatever it was, it wasn't something he wanted to feel. Numbness and guilt were comforting, reminding him again he didn't deserve to feel anything else. He should leave Buck and Megan to their cozy cookie-making. Yet he couldn't make himself go, not when Megan's laughter was like brilliant light, forcing its way into his darkness.

"Noah, would you mind helping me with this oven? I think there is something wrong with the door," Buck said.

Noah sighed, crossing the room. "Sure, Buck, let me take a look at it."

He pulled open the oven door, the hinge grinding and then coming to a halt. Moving closer, he inspected the rusted hinge at the joint of the two metal arms and the nut holding them together. "Yup, looks like the hinge is busted from overuse. Do you have a screwdriver nearby? I can bypass the screw so that its usable until you can get a new arm."

A scrabble in another draw followed, and Buck fished out a medium-sized flathead screwdriver. Noah quickly undid the screw, enabling the two arms to slide past each other and allowing the oven door to close.

"That should work for a little while," he said, opening and closing the oven door again.

"Thank you. What temperature did that recipe book say, Megan?" Buck asked.

"Three seventy-five. Don't worry about that anytime soon. The dough will need to rest for an hour before we can roll it out for the cookies."

"Ah, I leave you to it then," he said and quit the room.

Noah didn't know whether he should follow Buck when the only thing he really wanted to do was be near Megan and feel that strange emotion she invoked in him. *You're treading a dangerous path, Noah Thomas,* he thought. He knew he was; but in this moment, he didn't mind.

"Megan, right?" he asked, finding himself doing the very thing he'd told himself he wouldn't do—engaging in conversation with her.

"Noah, right?" Megan replied.

He chuckled. "Got it in one. What brings you out this far on a day like this?"

Her hands flipping pages of the recipe book paused as she replied, "I had to visit my professor." She shrugged. "There was an overdue paper and a situation I had no way around."

When she went silent, he waited for her to continue. A long minute passed. "What is the situation?" It was inexcusable, really, him asking this question. Her life had nothing to do with him; and if his thinking was in the right place, he would keep it that way.

"Are you always this inquisitive?" she asked, turning her attention back to the recipe book.

"As a matter of fact, no."

Her hands paused again, and she exhaled heavily, "My brother Tyreke's wife, Mia—her father, Mr. Ambrose, was diagnosed with Stage Four cancer this week. I had a paper due and didn't get it in on time." She swallowed hard.

He wanted to go to her and help her somehow, but what could he do? He could barely keep himself going most days. What did he have to offer her? Nothing. That was what.

"I'm sorry. Forget I asked," he said. He turned to leave, only to be brought up short.

"Do you want to help me with these cookies?"

Chapter Eight

"I . . . ah . . . sure," Noah said pensively, like it was really the last thing he wanted to.

That didn't surprise her. Since she'd spotted him on the other side of the threshold, his body language had made it clear he did not want to be in same room as her. Why was that? Was it that she'd witnessed something that made him uncomfortable? Compassion squeezed her heart as she watched the tall, strong man on the other end of the kitchen. An injury like the one Noah had experienced was bound to have some psychological implications. Isn't that what all her textbooks said?

"I mean, if you like. It's okay if you don't want to help," Megan ended softly. Taking the recipe firmly in hand, she gathered the ingredients for the cookies from the pantry cupboard, aware of the eyes following her every step. This would be awkward. "Really, I can do it on my own."

"I don't mind," Noah said, crossing the room toward her. His body was stiff, his eyes filled with resolve, like he was marching into a battlefield instead of crossing a kitchen to make cookies. He looked uncomfortable, and she wondered why he had agreed to help.

At his agreement, her stomach did that whoop thing again, her nerves tingling to life. He roughly cleared his throat and came to stand beside her,

"I can't say I have much experience with making cookies. You'll have to show me how."

"It's not that difficult—simple, really. Add everything together, mix, freeze for an hour, and then cut and bake. Easy as pie." She chuckled at her own joke, admiring the sound of his short, amused snort. There was only a hint of smile on his lips, and it did plenty to make those nerves dance.

"Sounds like something even I can't screw up," he said.

Quicker than she'd had a moment to notice, his jovial expression fell into one of abject misery. What had happened?

Megan paused her measuring and dumping, searching his face. Had he meant to say that? She let out a sigh. "Yes, well." And unable to fathom the emotion flitting across his face, she returned to study the last few ingredients needed. She handed a cup of brown sugar and measure of molasses to Noah to dump into the mixer.

He smiled again; it was small and, by the darkness in his eyes, took some effort to produce. She couldn't help but smile back, noting some of the darkness lift. As the gingerbread cookie dough churned together in the mixture, Megan leaned against the counter to study Noah.

"Why did you say it like that?" she found herself asking.

A cup of coffee lifted midway to his mouth, Noah paused, clearly surprised by her question. "No reason," he said, shrugging.

There was more to it. She knew it. *Leave it alone, Megan.* If Noah wanted her to know his business, he would tell her without her having to pry it from him.

Aware of this and ignoring her own advice, she spoke, anyway. "In my studies, I have found that usually when a person says something so cryptic, there is some story behind their words."

A deep frown bent his forehead; and he inhaled sharply, uncomfortable with her assessment. Noah turned his back on her, tension lining the broad expanse of his shoulders, and put the distance of the kitchen between them. Long minutes of silence followed.

Megan turned her attention back to the cookies, regretting her untimely nosing into his business. She hadn't meant to put Noah on guard. Maybe it was the lack of sleep talking or the relief of the long day and her assignment problem finally being solved. Whatever it was, she knew she should tread lightly when talking about the past with him.

Abruptly, he turned to face her, his knuckles white around the coffee cup in the intensity of his grip.

"Oh, and what are you studying?" His tone was hard, his expression mocking. Pain swept off him in waves, darkness burning in the depths of his gaze. She didn't fear for her safety, only felt a deep compassion for what she recognized as grief.

"Psychology," she said and wanted to continue; however, if possible, his expression became harder.

"Figures," he said, setting the empty coffee mug down on the counter with a little more force than necessary. "What made you want to do that? Wanting to solve the world's problems?" There was no kindness in his words, only bitterness and hurt.

She stiffened, straightening to her full height. He didn't scare her; years of being a baby sister had taught her enough to stand up for herself.

"Some people find it very therapeutic to talk to someone when they are facing a situation. It helps them to deal with the pain of losing someone they love."

"What about you? Do you think talking about your feelings makes a sudden loss bearable?" It wasn't what he said that told her how much he was hurting but the string of aching emotions threading across his face. "Talking just brings everything you want to forget to the forefront of your mind. It's easier to leave it in the past."

A part of her agreed. After all, wasn't she herself wary of dealing with the past? Yet she quickly shook her head, turning the switch of the mixer to drown out the possibility of further conversation.

Minutes later with dough complete, she turned the mixer off, accepting that if she was going to be of any help to this man, she needed to be honest. There was no reason to hide why she'd chosen psychology, but what was it that made her want to tell this man anything about her? Was it the anguish she saw in his eyes? Or the way his sadness resounded with her own sore heart?

"Three years ago, my parents died in a boating accident." She swallowed. "It was the night my brother Tyreke and Mia got married. After they'd left for their honeymoon, my parents were taking a moonlit sail." She hadn't been there, too busy with the other bridesmaids and caterers cleaning up after the wedding. "There was an unexpected storm. We don't know what happened—only that the next morning, they were gone."

Reaching up to wipe the tears from her face, she continued, "I was going to be a journalist. That day changed all I knew. It put me on my current path. Psychology seemed like a good choice to understand my own emotions and process my grief. It did for a while. Last week, we heard about Mr. Ambrose; and I knew my family would need me. My choice of career would benefit them, too." Her next words stuck in her chest when she saw his harsh features begin to soften.

"Makes sense, I guess. I'm sorry for your loss. It must have been a very hard time." He moved back to stand beside her, silently sharing her pain. But what about him? Did she dare ask?

"What about you? What are you grieving?"

It was a very bold thing to say; and she was sure he wouldn't answer, judging by the denial that immediately displayed itself on his face. It had come right after a quickly hidden flash of sadness and pain. She lifted the mixer's head and tipped the dough onto the counter, rolling it into a flat circle before wrapping it carefully in cellophane and placing it on the top shelf of the fridge.

On her journey back across the kitchen to the coffee station, Noah turned and left the room. Megan paused, dragging her hands through her hair. She stared at the empty doorway thoughtfully. It wasn't so much the fact that he had stormed out of the room that pinched her heart; it was the expression on his face and the defensive hunch of his shoulders. What burden was Noah carrying that made a proud and strong man turn into himself with pain?

Her mind turned over situation after situation as she busied herself with cleaning. Was it a family member he grieved? A wife? A girlfriend? Did it have to do with his leg? And why did she find herself wanting to know everything about him? What was it about him that seemed to have all her attention from the moment she'd met him yesterday? The minute oven timer ticked over thirty times as she stood back resting against the kitchen counter unseeingly, staring at the space around her.

Male voices coming nearer drew her out of her thoughts. "I think when the snow lets up, we will go to the back lot. There are older trees there that might need to be cleared out to make space for the younger saplings."

Buck walked back into the kitchen, heading straight for the coffee machine, oblivious of the tension that entered the room with Noah. Megan opened the fridge door and pressed the chilled dough between her fingers. Ice-cold and harder than earlier, the dough was ready to be shaped for the cookies. Moving the round of dough to the now-clean counter, she searched around for a rolling pin. "Buck, where is the rolling pin?"

"In the cupboard over there," Buck said, gesturing to a row of upper-level cupboards beside where Noah stood shoulder pressed against the door frame. His face was set in a bland mask, arms crossed over his chest; his feet set were the only display of his unease. A flutter of nerves twisted Megan's stomach at his defensive posture as she brushed past him to reach the cupboard.

"Excuse me," she whispered.

Noah spared her a glance and then moved out of way, making no effort to help. Oh boy, she had really done it now. Oddly, she didn't regret it because it was clear to her—although perhaps not to Noah himself—that he needed someone to talk to. Megan wouldn't normally offer herself; but seeing as they were stuck here, she might be the only one around who would listen.

"Thank you," she said, retrieving the baking instrument and beginning the process of rolling the dough until it was soft enough to be shaped and then baked. Buck and Noah's conversation about trees continued. Megan listened with half an ear, noticing the way Noah respectfully deferred to the older man, adding his opinion only when asked for it. There was something authoritative in the way Noah spoke, like he was a man used to giving orders—or had been, at some point.

Her eyes swept up again, her breath catching in her chest when she caught Noah watching her. She'd been so busy with the process of making cookies, hoping it would take her mind from the man she had no business thinking about, that his perusal had skipped her notice. Her hands trembled as she lifted each cookie cut-out and placed it in the trays she'd prepared earlier, ready for the oven. The trembling intensified as the clop of boots crossing a room grew louder—one set of boots leaving, one set drawing closer to her.

"I'm sorry about earlier," Noah said in a low voice.

An apology? That she hadn't expected. What had she expected? Stilted silence?

"No, I am sorry. Its none of my business." Her heart went into overdrive as work-roughened hands covered hers, pausing her rolling. Her heart ricocheted around her chest; and she swallowed hard, lifting her head to meet his gaze. Warmth infused her body as when it caught and held.

Noah shook his head, the gentle smile she'd seen yesterday hovering over his lips. "It's only natural to ask. I was intrusive enough to ask about your life." He let go of her hands and moved beside her, giving her space. "My wife," he said suddenly, eyes downcast at his hands, "she's the one I still grieve." When he didn't continue, it was hard not to ask questions; but she could respect when someone was not ready to talk about something.

"Can you open the oven for me? It should be ready." She handed him two of the four trays, sliding the first two onto the top shelf and then the others onto the bottom.

Noah pressed down on the arm of the oven, and the door closed with a gentle slap. "It was all my fault."

Chapter Nine

"What happened?" Megan asked.

What was he thinking? Noah ran his hand through his hair, absently rubbing the side where he'd broken a few ribs during the accident. This was a bad idea. He'd known it the moment he'd seen Megan at the door seeking shelter from the storm. What was it about this woman that made him want to spill all the secrets he'd kept from everyone—everyone, that is, that didn't know him as well as his brothers? He reminded himself of all the reasons getting more involved with Megan was a bad idea; however, there was a part of him—a small part—that wanted to tell her, if only to let her know he understood her pain.

Megan turned from the oven and, as before, did not ask, although her warm eyes filled with compassion. There it was again, the understanding and the sadness. She knew pain and grief just like he did—with one glaring difference. Her grief came from genuine sadness at loss, his from guilt and self-pity. How did the two juxtapose into understanding?

"Teneal was my high school sweetheart," he said. Once the box those wounds were held in opened, everything flowed out. "All I've ever wanted was to be a soldier; so when I enlisted out of high school, we married. For my first few tours, although long, things between us were going well. Teneal had gone to college to study marketing and was working in a job she loved."

He wanted to stop speaking before all the good memories came to the crashing inevitable end, as he knew they would. "Until one day, a few years later, I circled back; and she was gone."

He cleared his throat, trying to push aside his emotions at the way her letter had torn into him. "I went looking for her, knowing she hadn't gone far—the one and only time I ever got behind the wheel of a car with no intention of being safe. Considering the forecast for that day, I should've been more careful."

Megan's expression didn't change; the compassion in her eyes held. And still, she didn't say anything, merely waited for him to finish. It was a small mercy.

Gathering his courage, he pressed on. "We were on our way home to talk, the storm raging on." He'd been driving too fast and could still hear the sound of the other truck—screaming tires, blaring horn, and the horrible screech of metal as the truck hit them, pushing them into the forest. "A car wreck," he said, gesturing to his leg. "Cost me a leg, cost Teneal her life."

The emotion of that night assaulted him in living color. The next morning, he'd woken damaged, half the man he used to be, and carrying the knowledge that he had killed his wife. His stupidity had cost him more than he'd ever been willing to pay to have her back. Heat filled his eyes. He swallowed hard; he didn't deserve the solace of tears, not for what he'd done.

A gentle hand rested on his shoulder; it was warm , the heat of the kitchen forgotten against the frigidity of his memories. How would he ever forgive himself for what he done, what he had caused?

Teneal's father still hated him for taking his daughter. His hatred was small compared to the intense hatred Noah held for himself.

"Noah?" Megan whispered.

He couldn't lift his gaze; shame hot and burning like acid in his gut ate at him, the memory of that night ripping into the places he'd thought had been healed over. When would he be able to think of that night and not bleed on the inside? Never would not be long enough.

"Noah." Megan's hand fell softly on his, wrapping around his shaking fingers. "I'm so sorry, Noah."

He didn't deserve her sympathy or the compassion and knowing he found in her eyes. Gently removing his hand from under hers, he straightened. "Don't feel sorry for me, Megan. It was my fault. I didn't deserve her, and I don't deserve a lovely girl like you trying to help."

Anger lit those brown depths, fire lingering in them. "That's not true, Noah. Everyone deserves compassion; everyone deserves to grieve. Mistakes aren't the decider of the rest of our lives."

He hardened his heart against her words. Funny that Levi had said the same thing to him—perhaps not in the same words, but the message was the same. Forgiveness would bring an end to his pain. But like the time Levi had said them, Noah pushed them from his mind and heart just like he would do here.

"You're young, Megan." It was the insult he'd meant it to be, and he could see it take effect. "Idealistic. Not everyone thinks like you." He said the words with as much scorn as he could muster, hoping they would be enough to drive away her sympathy. Let her see that there was nothing worth saving when it came to him, nothing to be done to heal his pain.

She didn't flinch, the fire gentling to embers. "At least I'm old enough not to hide behind my mistakes instead of dealing with them. I'm not going through my life feeling sorry for myself."

If she had slashed him with his field knife, the wound would have hurt less because her words were true. It stung that someone who barely knew him could so accurately describe his state of mind. He wanted to leave, to run; however, that would only give credibility to her words. She was right; and he knew it, which didn't mean he had to like it. Luckily, the decision was taken from him.

"Am I interrupting something?" Buck asked, sticking his head into the doorway, wariness coloring his features.

Noah immediately flinched back. What was he doing? he thought, realizing how close Megan and he were standing, having moved during the course of their conversation. "Nothing, Buck. I think I'm going to check how the storm is coming along."

It was the easy way out and gave Megan no recourse; anything she said would only make an already awkward situation more so. Lengthening his stride to get out of the room quicker, he fled.

Just like him, wasn't it?

Turning to follow Noah, Buck glanced back at her, his expression perplexed. Megan stared back, unsure of what to make of Noah's exit either.

Buck sighed. "I better make sure he doesn't do anything stupid."

Megan nodded, not knowing how to respond. What had made her say those things to Noah? What was the matter with her? If anyone could understand how grief affected people, it was her. Sometimes, it was easier to leave it in the past, ignore it, and hope that some day to come to peace with it. She was sure Noah had relived that night again and again until he had tortured himself into the dark place he seemed to prefer to stay.

She'd been there when her parents passed. She'd been in that dark spot and had fought with everything in her to climb out. There were days she succeeded and days like three days ago when the weight of her grief would overcome her. But she'd fought back. Why hadn't Noah? Had the death of his wife impacted him to the extent that he didn't see his way past it? She guessed their aforementioned conversation gave her an answer to that.

Maybe the better question was what would make him reach for the peace he so obviously needed? He was older and, she was sure, had seen more of life than she ever had. Why had he not fought against the darkness? Was it his guilt that held him there? He had said it was his fault the accident had happened, but was there more to it?

Glancing again at the empty doorway, she sighed. No answers would come today. Megan leaned against the counter again, waiting for the timer to complete its cycle around the little round face, lost in thought. When the cookies had baked and cooled, she quickly packed them in an airtight container. There wouldn't be time to ice them, and this was the best she could do given the amount of time that had passed already. It was high time to do her own check on the storm.

Megan leaned closer to the window, watching the light cloud of flurries floating down onto the densely packed snow. True to Buck's estimation, the storm was lifting; and already in the distance, glimpses of the blue sky were emerging. A pathway down the drive of the farm had already been cleared, and she didn't have to think hard of who had been responsible for the plowing. She hadn't seen hide nor hair of Noah since he'd stalked from the kitchen.

Washing her hands again, she wiped them dry and pulled out her phone. No bars. She opened her messenger app anyway and shot a message to Grace at Snow Town Coffee that she was leaving soon and would be at the shop as soon as possible. The message would go through as soon as her phone connected to the network outside of town.

"Buck," she said, entering the study.

Buck sat, stretched out, with his ankles crossed in a leather chair, a book open on his lap. His eyes were closed, and his chest rose in a gentle rhythm. Megan smiled at the peaceful picture. Collecting the sealed cookie container from the kitchen, she placed it on the table beside him and wrote a small note.

Buck,

Thank you for sheltering me in the storm. Here are your cookies as promised.

Megan

She left the note on the lid of the container, slipped on her jacket, and gathered the rest of her things. Her messenger app pinged quietly as the text to Grace went through, and Megan sighed in relief. Leaving the house through the door she'd come in, she jolted to a stop at the sight of Noah leaning over the hood of her car, clearing the thick layer of snow that had accumulated there from the storm. He must've heard her gasp because he paused for a moment, looked at her, and then continued on with the task he'd assigned himself.

"I'm almost done," he said quietly. "You should be able to leave soon."

There was an unfathomable emotion in his voice again that Megan did not know how to react to. Another apology? Blinking slowly, she descended the steps, crossing the snow to her car.

"Noah . . . " What did one say in a situation like this? Yes, she was thankful that he'd helped her with the snow, but what of all that had taken place inside the house? How did she approach this awkwardness between them? "Thank you," she said. "I don't know if I would have been able to dig it out by myself."

He gazed at her a long time, his mouth opening and closing once, twice as if he, too, struggled to find words to speak, then sighed softly and rubbed the back of his neck.

"You're welcome." His smile was genuine, a little stiff like his shoulders, softened by the small bend in his lips. "You take care driving back to town. I'm not sure if the roads have been plowed yet."

"I will and thank you again. Please tell Buck I really appreciate the stop-over."

There was an awkward silence while she walked closer to him. She stared into his blue eyes, fascinated by him.

"Will do," he said roughly, clearing his throat.

Heart filled with questions, Megan waved one last time, climbed into her car, and drove toward town, glancing more than once to the man in her review mirror. The silence was broken by the loud procession of her ringtone. She lifted her phone to her ear.

"Mia, what—"

"Megan, how quickly can you make it to the hospital?"

Chapter Ten

"One more rep. Come on, soldier, push it." An army vet in his own right, Brett Morris, his physical therapist, had all the tenacity of a drill sergeant and none of the compassion.

Never mind the fact that the rehabilitation center at Snowy Medical Hospital was Noah's least favorite place in the world. It wasn't so much the fact that the hospital was in Snowy Springs; it was the idea of it, the smell of it, and the memories. Those often were the hardest to work through.

Sweat dripped down Noah's face; his arms shook with fatigue; his legs leveled against the parallel bars to his left and right, muscles straining as he worked. Although wielding an axe and chainsaw took a large amount of energy, strengthening the damaged muscles of his leg while bearing all of his body weight took just about everything he had left. He drew in two more deep breaths, lifting the dead weight attached to his leg one more time. Physical therapy was more grueling than basic training.

"Okay, one more rep at the leg press and then to the pool," Brett said, taking in Noah's soaking form with a practiced eye. "A week or two of this, and soon I'll be able to see you once a month."

"Thanks," Noah said sardonically. "If I make it that far." He grinned as Brett laughed.

"You're doing great, Noah." Brett held out a hand towel to Noah; and he gratefully accepted it, wiping his face. He sucked down the contents of his water bottle and sighed as Brett released the weight on his leg and led him over to the leg press.

"How's the leg feeling?" Brett asked as Noah sat down. He bent over Noah's stump, inspecting the skin where the limb met the prosthesis.

"The phantom pains and muscle spasms that come at night are a killer." He grimaced, remembering the pain he'd been in the night before. "Especially on days when I am on my feet for long periods of time."

His words were cut of by an agonizing cramp ripping through his leg. He gasped, gritting his teeth against the assault. Brett, already close by, removed Noah's prosthetic leg and gently massaged the scarred, bandaged-covered flesh until, at last, the aching muscle relaxed. Several deep breaths passed between Noah's lips before he slumped back into the bench worn out by the onslaught. Six months after the accident and he could still hear the screeching of tires and the deafening bang that had stopped their trajectory every time he looked at his leg.

He cleared his throat, sucked in another breath, and swallowed hard against the memory. Would it ever end? Would he ever be normal again? Or would he be stuck in a cycle of pain and grief for the rest of his days? He rubbed his eyes tiredly, staring morosely at the linoleum floor by his one good foot, feeling sorry for himself.

There was a moment of humor as he remembered Megan's words, knowing how right she was. He was feeling sorry for himself, but what could he do about it? He got up in the morning, went to work, lived—or so he thought. Was he really living or just existing?

Another good question he didn't really want to look too closely at. And what was it about Megan Davis that had brought on this need for introspection? He'd been just fine in his own suffering, and there she was showing him a standard he didn't think he could reach. The next question was, however, did he want to?

"You ready for the pool?" Brett asked, helping Noah up from the exercise bench and guiding him to his feet. Bracing Noah against his lower back, Brett helped him to the pool across from the therapy room.

"Today, I would like you to work on your stretches. The increased flexibility in your muscles and tendons will help with those spasms."

Noah nodded, slipping gratefully into the warm water. He pushed his confusing thoughts into the back of his mind to contemplate another time. The gentle pressure and heat massaged his tired muscles, and he felt himself slowly relax. He lay back, floating for a few moments, mind empty, body at rest, and Megan's beautiful face behind his closed eyelids. What was he doing? Moving to stand, he focused himself on his stretches and hoped it would be enough to keep his mind where it should be—in the therapy pool doing stretches. It worked, mostly.

Thirty minutes later, Noah balanced under the hot spray of the showers, the pressure kneading the tired muscles of his neck and back. His body felt more relaxed; however, his mind seemed determined to harp on all Megan had said. Freshly showered, he sat staring blankly at the dressing room floor, his mind wandering around in circles. Thoughts of Teneal, Levi, and Michael spun like a film on repeat.

He continued to sit. He should get up and get dressed, but he couldn't find the energy. Where was the sense of accomplishment he should feel at his progress today? There was only a hollow sense of emptiness and an ache he didn't like. A sigh slipped between his lips. Why now? Why did he keep thinking of this?

He knew, although he didn't want to admit it to himself. Since circumstances had brought Megan Davis into his life, he'd found himself thinking, wondering, and dreaming. Dreaming? He snorted. Of what? What did he want? His attraction to her frightened him; and despite the bullish way he'd handled her this afternoon, she'd still managed to get him to spill his guts about his marriage and Teneal—something only Michael and Levi knew. No, even if circumstances brought them together again, he had to keep his distance, more so for Megan's sake than for his own. He was not good enough for a woman like Megan. Hadn't his failed marriage already proven that? Noah Thomas was not relationship material, and that was that.

Blowing out another breath, he squeezed the bridge of his nose and shivered. The air around him, cool and filled with condensation, sent ripples of goosebumps over his flesh. He reached for his prosthesis, fitting it to his wrapped stump, and pulled on his clothes. Pants, shirts, sweater in quick succession were followed by socks and shoes. His stomach grumbled loudly. Figures, after missing lunch because of cookie-making and then clearing Megan's car, he hadn't had anything to eat since breakfast; and he was starving. Hospital cafeteria food wasn't the best; but as hungry as he was, he doubted he would notice the difference.

Treading carefully over the slick floor, Noah made his way from the changing room to the elevator. He pressed the button for the first floor, where the cafeteria was, and waited as the elevator descended. Large metal doors chimed and opened, allowing him to exit.

Noah scanned the metal tables of the cafeteria. Many were filled with people chatting quietly under the strains of classical music playing from the speakers placed in two corners of the room. He jerked to a stop, blinking hard.

There, across the room, stood the very woman he'd spent the better part of the last two days trying to erase from his mind. Then he noticed Megan's posture; it was hunched over with her arms wrapped around her waist, eyes blinking furiously. What was the matter? Immediately, he fought the urge to go to her, stopping himself in time to remember his decision. Noah turned to leave. He would get food somewhere else.

His gaze lingered on her long enough to see Megan wipe the small droplets racing over the smooth skin of her cheek. His resolve crumbled. What it was that pulled him to her he'd never know; but six longs strides later, he was beside her, hand stretched out to touch her shoulder and fighting the urge to take her into his arms.

Chapter Eleven

She should have known he would appear. Megan jumped as a warm hand landed on her shoulder.

"Hey," Noah said softly. "Are you okay?"

"Yes," she sniffed. "I mean, no."

Megan tried to clear the pain from her chest, swallowing hard. She turned to face him, noting he was so much closer than she expected him to be. The warmth of his body and familiar scent were oddly comforting. What little composure she'd managed to muster as she walked out of Mr. Ambrose's room a few minutes ago broke, and her tears ran freely. The treatment would not work. Mr. Ambrose's cancer was too advanced, and all Dr. Brouwer could promise was that the chemo would extent his life for a little while.

The stabbing ache in her chest pierced her again as she thought of Mia, Tyreke, and Isaiah. She could be brave for them—and would be brave for them, even when it felt like her insides were being ripped out a second time. Fat droplets ran down her cheeks as the façade she'd kept in place for her family fell away. Tentatively, two strong arms surrounded her pulling her into a warm, muscular chest. He held her tight, one hand running up and down her back, soothing and comforting. She allowed herself to relax fully into his embrace.

Noah sighed, brushing her cheek with his and whispered, "I've got you. Let it out. I'm here."

She let him hold her because there was no one to be brave for her in this devastation. A stranger, yet not a stranger anymore. They shared something in common, something they both carried with them from the past—a shared grief, the connection between them formed from their time together that morning. Noah understood, and that was a comfort to Megan. Her heart settled; and she let herself cry, burrowing into the soft material of his shirt, allowing herself the comfort of his hug.

When her sorrow began to ebb, Noah handed her a travel pack of tissues and led her to a nearby table. The table was booth-like, allowing Noah to shift in beside her as they sat down, resuming their embrace. She didn't move away.

"Better?" he asked, taking another tissue from the pack and handing it to her.

"Yes, as well as can be expected." She wiped her face and drew a few deep breaths.

"What happened? I assume it wasn't my sudden appearance that made you cry?"

His joke fell flat, although Megan appreciated the effort.

"No." She tried to smile and failed miserably. "The treatment isn't going to work," she began. "The doctors say they can't do anything for Mr. Ambrose. It's too late."

"I'm sorry, Megan." Compassion leaked from every word. "That must be really hard." Something brushed the top of her head as he pressed her closer. "When did you get here?"

"Mia called me from the road. He went for his first round of chemo today and isn't feeling very well. Dr. Brouwer says he is reacting badly, and they want to keep him overnight to make sure nothing else happens."

Noah's fingers wrapped around her hand, squeezing gently. Her heart stuttered in her chest, even though she knew he wished only to reassure her. Her head demanded she move away, break his embrace, and create some distance between them as this could only lead to confusion. So why didn't she? Why did she just sit there breathing in his comforting scent and allowing the warmth of his body to thaw the cold in hers? She needed an anchor, someone to hold onto her while the storm that reminded her of her own parents' passing raged around her. She needed someone; and he, for reasons she could not understand, was here being that someone for her.

"Megan?" Mia's voice startled Megan out of her musing. "Oh, thank goodness, I was looking for you everywhere . . . " Her voice trailed off with a gasp, seeing Noah for the first time, his arm wrapped around her. "Oh . . . who is this?"

Megan turned toward her sister-in-law, heat filling her cheeks.

"Mia." Megan rose, feeling bereft at the loss of Noah's warmth beside her. Putting some distance between them, she stood beside her sister-in-law. Logic told her there was nothing here to be embarrassed about, although she supposed that was not the reason her cheeks felt so hot, as if she had sunburn. Noah glanced up in amusement.

"This is Noah Thomas. He's . . . ." What did she call him? They weren't even friends. Were they? Her gaze connected with Noah's, and she felt her cheeks get hotter. He raised an eyebrow in question, leaning back into the booth relaxed and smiling. She shrugged. How did she put a name on something if she didn't know what it was?

Noah's smile widened, and he nodded. "Noah Thomas," he said, rising and extending a hand to shake Mia's hand. "Megan and I are recent friends."

It was almost said as a challenge—as if she would refute it. She looked into his eyes and saw only amusement and kindness. Gratitude and something like affection warmed her—so much so that she wanted to close the distance between them if only to feel his warmth close to her again. *Whoa, Megan, what is going on with you?*

"Yes, a friend," she said. "He's at the hospital for . . . " She stopped, realizing that she had no idea why Noah was at the hospital today. Coincidence? Maybe. Again, Noah had saved her from an awkward situation.

"Physical therapy." He gestured down to his leg, holding her gaze; and Megan understood. Of course, with his prosthetic limb, he would need therapy to learn how to walk normally again using the prosthetic.

He ran his hand through his messy, nut-brown hair, breaking their connection. She held back a sigh, heart thrumming inside her. Did he know how attractive he looked doing that? Her thoughts must have been clearly displayed on her face because Noah winked, flooding her face with heat again.

"I saw Megan at the coffee shop and came over to say hi."

It was so much more than that. If she was being honest with herself, Megan knew she was struggling to hold it all together; and as selfish as it sounded, it was nice to have someone who allowed her to borrow their strength for a while. Mia didn't need to know the real reason Noah had come to her aid. It would only worry her sister-in-law, and the last Megan wanted to do was add to Mia's stress.

"It's nice to meet you, Noah," Mia said, shaking Noah's hand. Her expression speculative.

"And you. Megan's sister-in-law, right?"

"Yes." Mia's eye widened. Megan held back a groan. There would be questions later—many questions as soon as Noah left. Megan had better come up with a good explanation as to why she was sitting in a cozy booth with a man Mia did not know about.

Mia moved away, walking closer to the counter to order coffee. Megan sighed quietly and then gasped in surprise when Noah took one of her hands into his. He drew her closer.

"I think that's my cue to leave," he said, bending close so she could hear his soft words. Whispers of electricity raced over her skin, starting at where his fingers held hers to where his voice lingered in her ears. He hesitated, his arms raising to enfold her again; then he stopped himself, aware that they had an audience.

"Are you going to be okay?"

"Yes, and thank you."

She would be lying if she didn't admit that being held by him again held so much appeal, she almost asked him for a hug. But that would lead to more confusion, and she didn't have enough to handle without adding that, too.

Noah seemed to know the same. His free hand clenched at his side as if he were restraining himself; he nodded once to Mia and squeezed Megan's hand again before releasing it.

"Goodbye, Megan," he said and lifted his backpack to his shoulder and walked toward the entrance of the hospital.

She watched him go. There was a finality she couldn't understand to his words.

"Bye," she whispered.

A grief different from the one she'd felt earlier squeezed her heart. It was silly, the things the mind brought up. Why would Noah be saying goodbye that way? It wasn't like she'd never see him again. Pushing aside the thought, she walked over to where Mia waited in the order line.

"Mia, look—" She didn't get further.

"Where did you meet that fine specimen of a man?" Mia asked. "Yummy. If I wasn't happily married . . ." She sighed, swooning with one hand pressed dramatically to her forehead.

Megan chuckled, her heart lighter after spending time with Noah and watching Mia's antics. Of course, Mia'd noticed how handsome Noah was; she'd have been blind not to. Did she notice how much older he was than Megan?

"Come on, spill."

"I met him yesterday. I had a flat, and Noah and his brother Michael were kind enough to stop and help me change it." She didn't mention earlier at Buck's farm when Noah and she had really gotten under each other's skin and learned things about each other that she doubted were shared with many people.

"Mmmhmm," Mia said. "Are you sure it's not more than that? You looked awfully cozy for two people who are practically strangers."

"Sometimes, once is all it takes," Megan said. What Mia didn't need to know was the feelings that came to life inside her when Noah was around—security, warmth, affection, a dire need to know him—really know him—and somehow be that same kind of person for him. She sensed he needed someone like that; and she, although not fit to be that person, found herself in the position.

Mia stepped forward to place her order with barista. "There's nothing wrong with making new friends," she said, a cheeky edge to her voice.

Megan decided to avoid the bait. "Of course." Nothing wrong at all.

"What are you having?" Mia asked, gesturing to the menu board. "I think I need a caramel latte. Tyreke said just black—how boring—and Mom wants tea . . . "

"I'll have a mocha, thanks," Megan said, taking a few bills from her purse.

Mia waved her away. "My treat—it's the least I could do after making you miss your shift today. I can still phone Grace if you need me to."

"No, don't worry. I explained when I called. Grace was very understanding."

"Good, I would hate to be the cause of you losing your job; you've already given so much for the family."

"It's hardly anything."

Mia turned to her, her expression sincere, and took Megan's hands in hers. "Trust me, Megs, it's not nothing. Tyreke and I really appreciate you looking after Isaiah and giving us the time we need to travel. I know the other night cost you a deadline for a paper, and I hope you can get an extension. You've worked so hard." Mia swallowed, her eyes welling with tears. "I can't tell you how much it means to my mother to have us here."

"Nowhere else I'd rather be," she said. "I spoke to my professor; thankfully, he, too, was understanding. He prayed for Mr. Ambrose and the family."

"How many times has Dad asked you to call him George?"

"More times than I can count."

"You know, I still don't understand why you don't call my dad by his first name. He thinks of you as a daughter, you know."

And in that was the problem. Megan knew Mr. Ambrose considered her and Tyreke like his own; but to Megan, it felt too much like replacing her own father—like if she called Mr. Ambrose by his first name, it would be like him taking over the memory of her dad. She'd tried to explain it to Tyreke, but he had insisted that it wasn't anything like that.

"I know," she conceded.

"Order for Mia." The barista's call interrupted anything else Mia might have wanted to add; and Megan was grateful for the reprieve, not only from the discussion about Noah but also from the discussion about Mr. Ambrose, too.

Together, they picked up the coffee and tea order and made their way toward the lift. Megan glanced once over her shoulder, surprised to see Noah leaning against a pillar outside the hospital entrance, his posture tense. What was he doing there?

Mia handed Megan her mocha, exchanging it for Tyreke's black coffee. She took a sip. "Thanks, this is good coffee,"

"For a hospital, they do have a good brand."

"Tell me about it."

They lapsed into silence as the lift rose to the third floor, each lost in thought.

Once they'd disembarked from the lift, Megan braced herself to return to Mr. Ambrose's room. She pushed aside her own fear and sorrow and thoughts of Noah to be there for her family. As expected, the room was quiet when they opened the door. Mia's father, attached to an IV drip and heart monitor, slept peacefully.

Mrs. Ambrose shooed them outside, gratefully accepting the tea that Mia offered. "He's finally fallen asleep; the doctors gave him something for nausea." She sighed heavily and took a sip of herbal tea, gesturing them to a nearby visitor's lounge.

"Thank you, I needed this," she said, taking one of the open seats by a large window. It overlooked the multitude of cars parked outside the hospital, snow dusting their windshield as it fell slowly down from the heavens.

"Where's Tyreke?" Megan asked, sure she had not seen her brother inside Mr. Ambrose's room.

"He went to fetch Isaiah from the daycare," Mia said, taking a drink from her own cup.

"What happened?" Megan asked, remembering the look on Mrs. Ambrose's face when her husband had suddenly gasped while in his bed and begun to shake furiously before emptying the contents of his stomach onto the floor. She and Mia had rushed from the room in search of a nurse. While Mia found an orderly asking for someone to help clean up the mess, Megan had escaped down the corridor to the coffee shop, afraid her panic would distract Mrs. Ambrose and Mia when they were needed most.

"A reaction to the medication for the cancer. Dr. Brouwer said this could happen; sometimes, patients have hypersensitivity to the drugs used for chemotherapy that can appear from minutes to hours after treatment. They will have to find something else to treat him." Mrs. Ambrose's old hands fluttered to her face as she covered it. They shook as she tried to lift the cup of tea and place it by her mouth.

"I don't know why God is allowing these things to happen to us, but I know He is still good," she whispered, her Mexican ancestry evident in her accent.

Megan wondered if she had meant to speak aloud so that she and Mia could hear.

Mrs. Ambrose closed her eyes, her mouth moving silently, tears running down her cheeks as she spoke. Mia shifted beside her mother, taking the hot teacup from Mrs. Ambrose and placing it on a nearby table with her own coffee. She curled her arm over her mother's shoulders, drawing her close.

Like an outsider, Megan sat and watched, unsure of what to do next. Did she join Mia beside her mother or just offer her silent support from across the room? There were some pains only family could understand. And despite the wonderful warm relationship Megan had with Mia's parents, they were not her parents; and she was not their child.

The constant ache she carried inside her intensified, and it took all her self-control to stop it from spilling over into her face. Mia and Mrs. Ambrose needed her. She would be there for them without falling apart, even when the picture of the two them together, sharing their confusions and grief, made her miss her own mom with an intensity that had her working her free hand into a fist to distract from the pain. Her grief could come later when she was alone and a burden to no one. So she set her coffee on a nearby table and held both their hands, offering what little comfort she could.

For a long moment, Mia and Mrs. Ambrose sat quietly beside each other, their tears falling in tandem with their prayers. The air around Megan lifted, filling with a soothing presence like a great hand, warm and solid, suddenly surrounding them.

Mrs. Ambrose smiled through her tears. "Yes, God is good."

Chapter Twelve

The cold weather outside slapped some sense into his fogged brain. Noah sighed and leaned against the icy outer wall of the hospital breathing deeply. It was probably good he had been unable to walk faster away from Megan, for it gave his heart time to settle into a more normal pattern than when she'd been beside him.

He groaned softly, adjusting the strap of his backpack on his shoulder, so it sat more comfortably on his tired muscles. What was he doing? Hadn't he told himself to stay away from Megan? And yet at the first opportunity that presented itself back into her life, he had leaped at it. What was worse, the feel of her in his arms was a memory that would not leave him anytime soon; and he wasn't sure whether he wanted it to or not. Her scent hung all around him, despite the stinging smell of antiseptic that lingered in the air at the hospital, and the memory of her soft curves melting into his.

He released a heavy breath. He should push that memory far from his mind. The way Megan made his blood flow was one thing, but he couldn't afford to think of her pressed against him. Holding her was a mistake. Wasn't it? Maybe there was still some kind of chivalry left in him; maybe he just had a giant hero complex; or maybe in that moment, he thought he could be someone better. In hindsight, he probably wasn't. Who took the advantage of holding a woman in her moment of grief? Noah knew it wasn't for attraction that he'd taken Megan into his arms. At least, it hadn't started out that way. He'd meant to comfort her only; however, her scent . . . He blew out another heavy breath.

And this was the reason he was outside in the cold, freezing his butt off instead of in the warm embrace of the hospital cafeteria eating the lunch he'd promised himself he would. It was strange to him the way the human mind worked, or maybe it was just the way his mind worked. He loved Teneal; and in the end, it had not been enough to keep her. If he hadn't been enough for a woman who promised to honor and cherish him until death parted them, he would not be enough for any woman.

Scowling yet unable to stop himself, he turned back to the hospital windows, hoping to catch a glimpse of Megan again. She was nowhere to be seen. Probably for the best. Being anywhere near her was driving him crazy; thinking of her made him think of nothing else and made him forget all the reasons he was in this mess to begin with.

Ice crackled beneath his boots as he crossed the slippery tarmac to where his truck waited. He glanced down at his wristwatch grimacing. He was late. Michael and Sarah were waiting for him at the Community Center fair for some family Christmas shopping. While the fair was not as big at the main big box stores in the neighboring towns, it had many unique stalls and gifts that were fitting for any Christmas gift. He'd promised Michael he would help choose a gift for Lana and Dakota; and right now, he was horribly late to keep his promise.

Stuffing the backpack in the back seat of his truck, he carefully climbed into the cab and turned the ignition. Twenty minutes later, he pulled into the aged parking space beside the Community Center, tugged on his woolen hat and gloves, and hurried into the barn-like interior of the Community Center.

Christmas exploded from every corner; upbeat Christmas songs rang from the mixture of speakers and voices in every corner. Lights hung in half-moon strings, lighting up the roof and stalls below. As he walked, he looked into the rooms surrounding the main area. Each one held a group of people engaged in various Christmas activities. One room held a group of children eagerly decorating gingerbread houses for the judges, circling them as they worked. In another room, he recognized the group of the woman from the church engaged in a quilt-making activity; and in another, circles of garland waited to be fitted with lights and tinsel the next day.

He found himself humming along with the Christmas songs and then stopped as soon as he realized he was singing the familiar words under his breath. What was going on with him? Before he had time to analyze his strange behavior further, Michael appeared with Sarah, Aaron, and Dakota in tow.

"Where have you been? I thought we agreed to meet at 4:30," Michael asked, his expression clouded and worried.

"Yeah, sorry I'm late, had some stuff to take care of. It couldn't be helped. Were you waiting long?"

"No, just ten minutes or so," Sarah replied, curling her arm around Michael's bicep, her engagement ring blinking in the twinkling white lights of the ceiling.

Michael looked down at her, his expression dopey. Noah looked up to see Aaron and Dakota sharing a private smile. All this sweetness was making his stomach twist. Maybe he shouldn't have agreed to come; all this mooning and longing was likely to rub off on him, and then he'd really be in trouble. For a moment, he wondered what it would be like for Megan to be here beside him, meeting up with his family; and together, they could Christmas shop. He shoved the thought away, once again reminding himself what a terrible idea it was.

Michael cleared his throat. "What couldn't be helped? Did your therapy session go over?" he asked.

Noah shook his head. It would be easy to tell the group that Brent had been ruthless today; but that would be lying, and lying never got anyone anywhere. He was not prepared to carry that weight with his overburdened conscience. "No, I ran into Megan at the hospital. She needed help with something." It wasn't his place to tell of the struggles currently facing her family, in that he would keep his answers as vague as possible.

"Ah." Michael grinned. "Megan needed help, interesting." His tone was suggestive; his grin widened into a full smile. Sarah and Dakota's gazes both flung to Noah.

"Megan, the lady you invited to church?" Sarah asked.

"Yes, the one Noah and I helped yesterday with her tire."

"How do you know Megan?" Sarah asked Noah.

Not for the first time did Noah wish he had kept his mouth shut and not mentioned Megan at all. Why hadn't he just gone for the easy out?

"It's a long story," he said.

"Oh, so there's a story," Aaron chimed in.

Noah groaned out loud. "A story which is none of your business."

By this time, Sarah and Dakota wore smiles to match their two significant others. Noah rubbed his hand down his face and then tucked his hands into the front pockets of his jeans.

"Are you here to shop or discuss my relationship with Megan?"

That stopped them all stiff. Noah scowled at his brother, who was doing nothing to hide his laughter. "That's not what I meant," he said sullenly.

Ignoring hand-covered chuckles from the rest of the group, Noah stormed over to the cookie and hot chocolate stand and ordered a large peppermint hot chocolate and a giant cranberry and white chocolate cookie. It would have to be enough to carry him until he could find some proper food for supper. Maybe he would go to Papa Paulo and get himself a meat and veggie supreme.

"I'm sorry, man," Michael said, coming to stand beside him. "It's just that hopeful expression on your face when you arrived is one I haven't seen for a long time. You look happy. I'm not going to ask if Megan was the one to put it there or if it's my imagination."

Noah shrugged. "It's fine, man. I wish I knew myself." That was a half-truth. He knew it was Megan who made him feel like he mattered when he held her, like she needed him; and if he were honest with himself, it felt good to be needed by someone, even if it couldn't last. Could it?

Michael let the subject drop when they were joined by the others, leaving Noah to contemplate the strange route his life had suddenly taken. Did he want this friendship with Megan to evolve into something more? His chest ached at the thought of their interactions coming to an end. Would he want their meetings to become more planned and less like fate was throwing them together in situations? And what was it she made him feel? Was there only attraction from his side? Or did she feel something similar when she was with him?

All he had were questions and more questions, and no answers were forthcoming. And so there was only one question left, really: was he going to do anything to make his friendship with Megan a more permanent fixture in both their lives? Or was he going to do what he'd promised himself to do when he'd first met her—stay away?

The conversation meandered to more normal things—Christmas gifts, the tree lighting the next week, and the Carols by Candlelight service being held in a week's time. Noah wandered around, sipping his hot chocolate and having munched his cookie faster than a wide receiver with an open field. Despite the size of the cookie, he was still starving. How much longer would Sarah and Dakota move from stall to stall looking at every little gift and ornament on offer, walk away only to return a half hour later, and purchase the first ones their hands had touched? Noah remembered shopping with Teneal. He expected the familiar ache is his chest to stab him again, it did but didn't hold the punch that usually accompanied such a memory.

Did that mean he was hopeful? Again, no answer came. Deciding the woman would no doubt be in the same spot for at least the foreseeable future, he followed his nose to the smell of warm, frying dough and cinnamon and sugar. Mrs. Delmonte, from the nearby bakery, stood behind a large frying pan; a large stringlike pastry dough in the shape of the number eight boiled rapidly in the oil. His stomach growled.

"Noah, how have you been?" Mrs. Delmonte asked. Her smile was wide and friendly, reminding Noah once again why he'd returned to Snowy Springs. It was like coming home. These people knew him and loved him, anyway.

"Very well, thanks. Can I have two please?"

Mrs. Delmonte handed over two pastries in exchange for the bills in Noah's hand.

"Keep the change," he said, mouth watering with the smell of warm cinnamon and sugar filling his nose.

"Enjoy," he heard Mrs. Delmonte say as he turned to leave. He shoved one of the warm, gooey pastries into his mouth and groaned quietly at how good they tasted, walking in the direction where he had last seen his shopping companions. As he passed a jewelry stall, a sparkling silver bracelet with a red stone caught his eye. He walked closer to the stall.

"Hi, Juliet," he said, greeting Sarah's best friend. "How is Callan?"

"He's very well, thanks. Keeping busy at the high school. You know that teaching teenagers is not an easy job."

Noah could only nod. "I suppose it's a lot like greenhorns in the army."

Juliet nodded, laughing. "How can I help you?"

He lay his bag of pastries beside him on the table looking down at the bracelet. "May I?"

"Sure." Juliet released the clasp on the bracelet, handing it to him. "The stone is genuine jasper; the bracelet is sterling silver."

The bracelet was delicate, its links sliding softly over his fingers, the gem at its center engraved with a single word: *hope*. He couldn't define the reason why it had drawn his attention, but he handed over the amount Juliet said and tucked the gift-wrapped item into his jacket pocket, picking up his cooled pastry and resuming his search.

Chapter Thirteen

"Love you, Isaiah," Megan said, quietly placing the sleeping infant in his pack-and-play and closing the door so only a sliver remained open. It was going to be another late night. Mr. Ambrose had rested peacefully for most of the afternoon; Mia and Mrs. Ambrose had sent her home with the hope she would get some rest. It wasn't an hour later when the phone call had come.

"Please, will you come and get Isaiah? Mom says Dad is reacting to the medicine again in a bad way. The doctor doesn't know what has caused it, and they are keeping him admitted longer for observation. Oh, Megs, he's so weak. I can't . . ." Tears muffled anything else Mia had to say; and five minutes later, Megan was on the road to the hospital to collect Isaiah from Mia and Tyreke.

She jolted out of her reverie as a soft but steady knock clapped against her apartment door. She glanced at the hall clock: 8:00 p.m. She grabbed her red hoodie, sliding it over her upper body, and quickly slipped on a warm pair of track pants from her closet. She hadn't been expecting anyone tonight. Everyone who would drop in at her apartment unannounced was at the hospital—well, almost everyone.

Megan breathed in deeply, hoping that whoever it was would leave quickly. Her mood did not want visitors, and she doubted she had the capacity to be congenial tonight. All she wanted was dinner and a good night's sleep.

"Who is it?" she asked, thinking about the last time her neighbor had needed her. Mrs. Greenably sometimes asked Megan to help her with whatever new tech her grandson had convinced her was essential for living. Often, the old lady had no clue how the home Alexa worked or how to find the contacts on her new cell phone; but she tried, anyway, as a way to stay connected with him. Megan appreciated the old lady's efforts and commended her for taking such an interest in the boy's life; but still, Mrs. Greenably always came at the most inconvenient times, and Megan never had the heart to turn her away.

There was a short pause before an answer came. "It's Noah."

Completely not the answer she was expecting. She glanced down at her outfit and shrugged. There was nothing to help it now—not that it mattered. If she went to change and left Noah in the hallway, it would inevitably lead to an embarrassing conversation about why she had taken so long to answer the door. That was one discussion she would very much like to avoid.

She tsked in annoyance. Since when did she care about such things? Its wasn't like Noah was here to pick her up for a date. Which begged the question, why was he here? Hoping her hair looked respectable in the messy knot she'd set it in while bathing Isaiah earlier, she pasted on a pleasant smile and opened the door.

Heat radiated through her chest at the sight that greeted her, reviving her sluggish heart rate to maximum warp. Noah Thomas, dressed in a casual blue flannel button down, a white crew neck peeking between its lapels; well-worn blue jeans; and a pair of sturdy boots was a sight to behold. His wild brown hair was neatly tamed and begged for fingers to be run through it. His dreamy smile had her struggling to keep her smile pleasant instead of transforming into one that made it obvious how gorgeous the man was. Did he know how his shirt brought out the blue of his eyes? They practically glowed. Megan swallowed hard, hoping that Noah couldn't hear the riot in her veins caused by his presence.

"N-Noah," she said, "how did you know where I lived?"

Noah shrugged, looking sheepish. "Well, it wasn't too difficult to find out. Process of elimination. When Michael and I changed your tire, you said you lived at Crystal Place. All I had to do was charm an old lady, Mrs. Greenably, into telling me which apartment was yours." Warm color filled his cheeks, and he absently shifted the wadded-up jacket hanging over his left arm. For a big, strong, scary man, he was adorable.

"Oh." It was understandable why the old lady who was a stickler for the apartment building rules would bend them for Noah. Any woman would be swayed by that smile and those gorgeous blue eyes—a smile that was focused on her and growing by the second. Did he know she was checking him out? And why wasn't he speaking? Why wasn't she speaking? Right, she should say something.

"Can I come in?" he asked quietly.

Heat filled her cheeks; and she quickly stepped back, allowing Noah entrance to her apartment. "Sure. Sorry, where are my manners? Come on in." Megan cupped her hot cheeks, grateful the frigid breeze that came from the hallway of her building for the first time.

"Thank you." Noah eyes swept the room as he crossed the threshold into the living room. What did he see? she wondered. However, when he turned back to face her, there was nothing but openness in his expression, an eyebrow raised. Right, toys and baby stuff. Noah handed her two stuffies as she hurried around the sofa collecting baby paraphernalia. Quickly dumping the toys into nearby hampers, she grabbed her coffee cup, along with Isaiah's bottle, and hurried them to the kitchen. Noah watched her every movement, his expression bemused. What was so funny? Wasn't he used to a woman running around her apartment in a desperate attempt to make it presentable?

"I seem to have caught you at a bad time," he said, amusement lacing his words.

"I wasn't exactly expecting anyone tonight; and with Isaiah here, I haven't had time to straighten things up."

"Then I am sorry to intrude. I can leave if you want."

Confusion met curiosity. "What?" She took a deep breath and then turned her attention fully on him, ignoring the twisted blanket on the sofa and the used spit-up towel hung over the top of the couch. "No, no, that won't be necessary. Just give me a minute to get rid of these things," she said, reaching for the towel.

Noah's hand stilled hers. "Really, I can come back another day," he said softly, sincerity burning in his words. There it was again—the uncertainty in his gaze, like he wasn't sure he should be there. Why had he come if he hadn't wanted to stay? Should she ask him to stay? It would be nice to have some adult company.

It wasn't just the company; Noah had been on her mind since the hospital and hadn't really left. Megan sat down on the sofa, ignoring the mess of fluffy polyester below her, and tapped the seat beside her, inviting him to do the same. An almost indecipherable relief flickered across his face before he tossed his jacket over the back of the couch and stiffly sat down.

"No, its all right. What can I do for you?" she asked.

Hands clasped easily between his knees, Noah glanced at her, focusing on her, trying, she thought, to see how his coming here would be accepted. He swallowed once and then straightened in his seat.

"First, how are you?"

Turned around and spun about by his presence at the moment—but she couldn't say that. "I'm doing okay, I guess."

Here the man was concerned for her, and she was trying her best to ignore how incredibly attractive he was.

"Mia and Tyreke are back at the hospital; I just got a text to say they would be there all night again."

Noah's expression changed to concern. "Maybe I should get going, then, leave you to your rest." He rose, collecting his jacket on his way back to the door.

"Noah," she said, stopping him, "why did you really come tonight?"

"I was wondering if I could take you out to dinner." His answer was quiet, and she could hear the uncertainty in his request.

Butterflies raced like tingles in her stomach. Dinner. He wanted to take her to dinner? Her surprise must have been evident on her face because Noah's expression tensed—hiding again. Megan braced herself for the brush off that would come; but he didn't move or say anything, just waited for her to turn him down. It wasn't that she wanted to, but there was so much going on in her life that she didn't have time to consider things like dating and romance. And then there was the age thing. Until this moment, Megan knew she could be friends with a man who was older than her; however, as soon as more came onto the table . . .

"I don't know if that would be good idea," she said softly, looking down at her hands.

"Okay." He drew a deep breath, kindness in his smile. "Why don't you tell me why you think so?"

Megan felt her cheeks heat. "Well, for one, you are quite a bit older than me, and two . . . "

Noah grunted something under his breath and sat down beside her. "Let me try that again. I would like to take you out as your friend. Both of us have had a rough time lately; and I thought it would be pleasant to enjoy a nice meal together, maybe see some Christmas lights or go to the market for an evening."

He curled his hand under her chin and lifted her face. "Just as friends, nothing more. Age doesn't matter with friends."

He released her chin, returning his hands to his lap. There was nothing but sincerity in his eyes, and she wondered if she had imagined the banked heat in his gaze. The emotion she felt in that moment confused her. She was, for lack of a better word, disappointed that Noah had made it clear that he only wanted to be her friend. In the next instant, she was grateful; his life and hers were complicated. She knew from their discussions the demons he fought, and she was trying to do her very best for her family without destroying her future. Complicated, indeed. Besides, if it was only dinner with a clear expectation in place, then why did she feel as if she was making the wrong decision?

"Tonight would be impossible. Another night perhaps?"

Noah smiled and rubbed his chin, considering her. "Sure, we can do that." He watched her for a long moment. What was he looking for? The silence stretched between them, tension filling the space where she ended and he began. His eyes warmed into liquid pools, hammering her blood through her veins. He blinked, releasing her, and cleared his throat with an easy smile on his lips. "Have you eaten yet?"

She shook her head. "No, I've been so busy with Isaiah that I haven't had time to get anything yet. I just put him down for the evening. Dinner was next in the plan."

"Okay, would you mind if I intrude on your evening for a little longer?"

Where was he going with this? And what of earlier? Wherever it was, it seemed to amuse him; and spending more time with him had its appeal.

"I don't mind," she said, unsure of what she was letting herself in for.

"Good, how about I order something from Papa Paulo's for us. You can find us one of those fluffy Christmas movies, and we can go out some other time."

Two dinners? She wasn't complaining. Despite the strange way her and Noah's paths had crossed, she was enjoying getting to know him better. They carried some of the same burdens, and she wouldn't quickly forget his gentle comfort that afternoon at the hospital. Although she was trying *very hard* to forget how he made her feel. Was it so bad that she wondered what it would be like to kiss him? Or what if they were more than friends?

"As friends?"

Noah raised his eyebrow. A wide smile lifted the corners of his mouth, a mouth she shouldn't be noticing and yet was wondering again about how his lips would feel pressed to hers.

"As friends," he said.

Chapter Fourteen

The tension in his chest eased considerably as Megan smiled and held out her hand to shake his, sealing their relationship status. He took it, allowing the wave of warmth from her skin to wash over his. Her skin was soft with callouses on the forefinger and thumb. Unsure of what the outcome would be when he decided to track her down, Noah was relieved that in the end, she had agreed to spend an evening with him.

"What kind of pizza do you like?" he asked, reluctant to let go of her hand. Megan didn't pull away. He did, though, because that was what friends did; and if he held it any longer, he would pull her into his arms again and give in to the desire to kiss her.

"Anything with meat on it, just not sausage," she said, curling her arms around her stomach as if she didn't know what to do with them. Was she as nervous as he was? Why was he nervous, aside from the obvious chance she would reject him? He wasn't here to take her on a date, although there was a part of him that would have liked to do just that. With his track record, it would probably end in disappointment for them both. There was chemistry between them; he felt it whenever they were in the same room. And judging by what had happened when he had arrived moments ago, it was not one-sided. Chemistry was not enough, though, and he knew that for a fact.

"My kind of girl," he said without thinking. He paused, waiting for Megan's response. She laughed and rose from the sofa, collecting the spit-up towel and blanket as she went.

"I'm gonna put these away while you call for pizza. Any specific preference of fluffy Christmas movies?"

"I'm not fussy." Truth was, he didn't remember the last time he'd sat down and watched a Christmas movie. Teneal hated those type of movies, preferring ones with action and a touch of romance. The only reason he'd thought to suggest it was because Sarah seemed to love them. He rubbed his chest, a heaviness suddenly settling behind his breastbone. When he thought back to near the end of their marriage, he and Teneal had rarely had a movie night. The drifting had started long before she'd left. In the six months before that fateful night, they had rarely been in the same room or company. He'd been deployed; and Teneal was busy growing her marketing company, always at one function or the other, networking. He'd missed the obvious signs.

Maybe you didn't want to see them. Was it true? Had he ignored the signals his marriage was falling apart? Why had Teneal never said anything? Did she think he wouldn't listen? Noah squeezed the bridge of nose, irritated with himself for having the moment of introspection. Was he wrong to want to spend an evening without the past getting in the way? His intention when seeking Megan out was to allow her to have an enjoyable evening. That was all, no other agenda. So why did he feel like he shouldn't be there? Like he should be at home with the curtains shut, sitting in darkness, mourning? But here he was in Megan's living room among her worn sofa pillows and Isaiah's baby paraphernalia. Why? Because there was something about Megan that made the darkness feel less heavy, and the miser that he was he wanted some of that light.

Megan paused at the entrance to the passage leading into the rest of the apartment. "Okay, I'll choose one when the food arrives."

"Sure." Noah flipped open the Papa Paulo's app on his phone and placed the order for two large meat surprise pizzas. He could hear Megan moving somewhere in the apartment just out of view. Pushing aside any other thoughts of Teneal, he rose and went to the kitchen in search of plates.

The kitchen was a mess. Dishes were spread across the pale beige countertops. Bottles and other baby supplies covered every surface. Two empty coffee cups sat in the sink, along with what looked like two days' worth of dishes. He smiled and shook his head, glad that Brady, Ben's son, was almost the same age as Isaiah and the little knowledge he had of babies could help Megan.

He ran the water and began to wash the bottles, stacking them on the drying rack one by one before placing them in the sterilizer and flipping the switch. Then he moved to the other dishes. By the time Megan reappeared, the kitchen was clean; and two large, hot pizzas waited on the counter. She halted in the entrance, her gaze bouncing around the room.

"You know you didn't have to clean my kitchen. I already said you could stay," she said dryly.

Not that he was noticing but she had changed her clothes, still casual but more suited for guests. He suppressed a smile; it was probably for the best that she'd changed because the soft track pants and sweater she'd been in earlier made him think of lazy mornings and late nights together. That was a place he could not allow his thoughts to go, as much as they wanted to.

"You never know, you could have changed your mind."

"Why would I do that? You promised to feed me. As a student, I never turn down free food."

And there it was again—the glaring difference between them, one of many.

"How old are you, Megan?"

"I thought age didn't matter in friendship," she quipped back.

He allowed his smile to widen. "It doesn't, but there seems to be some insurmountable obstacle attached to its value."

"Twenty-three. You?"

"Thirty-three." He braced himself, heart hammering in his chest. Would she reject him based on a number?

"Ah ha," she said, her brow creasing into a frown.

"It's not that big an age difference, you know." Who was he trying to convince—himself or Megan?

"No, I suppose not." She shrugged. What did it mean? Was she okay with them being friends, despite the ten-year difference? Choosing to shelf the question for the moment, he opened the nearest box of pizza. The smell of tomato, oregano, pepperoni, bacon, some other barbecued meat, and cheese filled the air.

"How about we get to the pizza before it gets cold?" he suggested.

"That sounds great. I'm starving."

He handed a plate to Megan, grabbed one of the boxes, and pointed to the living room.

"Did you decide on a movie?"

Megan eyed him a long moment and then nodded. "I found one with a naval officer and a girl trying to solve a mystery about a ballerina."

"Sounds good." Something caused his chest to clench. Was he ready to watch a movie that was set in the forces, even if it was sweet and fluffy? Bracing himself, he nodded. "I am sure it will be great."

"I can choose something else, if you like."

"Relax, Megan, what could be better than a navy ship and romance?" His tone was wry, bordering on sarcastic.

Megan laughed and turned to leave.

Together, they retook their seats on the sofa, and Megan began the movie. As soon as the opening credits rolled, he knew he should ask Megan to stop the movie. Memories assaulted him of his times in the forces, good and bad, culminating in the night he'd left base and would only return to collect his stuff to start his life as a civilian. He forced himself to chew his pizza, even though it tasted like ash on his tongue and sat like a wad of cotton in his throat.

Megan sighed softly, her piece of pizza forgotten on her plate. All his attention was on her, admiring the soft smile bending her lips as the two main characters learned about the missing ballerina, agreeing to work together to find her. His heart thudded painfully inside him; her beauty struck him afresh. Focused on Megan, he could forget about leaving a life he loved and learn to be satisfied with the life he had. He shoved another slice of pizza into his mouth, chewing quickly. The flavor hadn't improved, and it still sat in his throat. Megan came out of her daze and took a bite of her pizza.

"Enjoying the movie?" she asked. Her smile was wide and welcoming. The thought of taking the plate from her hands and closing the distance between them to find her lips burned through him. He gripped his plate a little tighter than necessary, suppressing the idea with lethal efficiency.

"It's all right—a little unrealistic, but not bad."

Could she tell how hard it was for him to sit beside her and watch the movie? It wasn't so much that it made him think of all he had lost; instead, it made him think of all he wanted. A friendship with Megan was a lukewarm offering to what he really wanted with her and could never have. He had to remember that; he had to keep his thoughts and hands to himself. He did keep his resolve for most of the movie; however, somewhere in the mix, he'd stretched his arm across the back of sofa, running a piece of Megan's hair idly between his two fingers. Megan didn't seem to notice anything, and that suited him just fine.

The movie was halfway over when he went to the kitchen to collect the second box of pizza, glad that Megan was eating with such gusto. She seemed a little more relaxed and was once again lost in the movie when he returned. He stood behind the sofa, watching her again as she giggled at something on the screen, the sound lifting some of the heaviness in his chest. Was he a fool? Maybe. Would he regret this night? Possibly. He should be home nursing his wounds; it was what he deserved after how his actions had ended Teneal's life.

But Megan needed someone. He could see the tiredness and creases of stress around her eyes and mouth, the way her shoulders seemed to be hunched in a defensive position as if bracing herself for the worst. He wondered if her family could see it, too. He resumed his seat, arm across the top of the sofa, concentrating more on Megan than the movie. It was almost done when a small but insistent whimper came from one of the rooms. Megan tensed and then sighed. He gently squeezed her shoulder.

"Isaiah?" he asked.

"He probably needs to be changed . . . " She pushed to stand up, and Noah gently tugged her down again.

"Sit. I don't know much about babies, but I know enough. I'll go see what he wants."

Her relief was palpable. Just how much strain was she under?

The whimper grew more persistent; and Noah went to the bedroom, lifting the warm little body from the camping cot.

"Hey, buddy, lets check out that diaper."

He braced Isaiah on the changing table, fumbling a bit to slide it under the little, wriggling body. It didn't take much practice; and although he'd done this a few times for Brady, he was by no means a master. A chuckle came from the door.

"Here, let me help," Megan held Isaiah's little hands in hers, while Noah quickly changed the diaper and snapped close the buttons of his onesie. He lifted Isaiah to his shoulder, taking the bottle from Megan's proffered hand.

"Go watch the end of the movie. I'll put him down."

Megan gazed at him for a long time before smiling softly. "Thank you," she said, trailing her hand from his shoulder to his hand, awakening a path of fire with her touch as she left the room. His stubborn, broken heart thudded inside him, pouring emotions into his body, emotions he had no right feeling or thinking about.

Sighing, he settled into the nearby chair and gave Isaiah his bottle. "Yup, buddy, I'm in trouble."

Chapter Fifteen

"Order up."

Megan hurried to collect the sandwich order from the pick-up counter, wiping her hands on her black apron as she went. Snow Town Coffee was bustling as it always was at this time of the day.

"Two Philly beef sandwiches with salad," Barb, the cook said.

"Thanks, B."

Warm from the heating tray, Megan carefully lifted the two plates and weaved her way between the customers to table three in the corner. Sarah Bakker and Dakota Manning sat with Lana Bakker, Sarah's mother, discussing Sarah and Michael's upcoming wedding.

"Two Philly cheese with salad; and Lana, your caramel cream pie is almost ready."

"Thanks," Sarah said, rising and taking the plates from Megan, placing one at her own place and handing the other to Dakota. The u-shape of the booth made it awkward for Megan to reach over Lana to get to Dakota's place.

Snow Town Coffee was in the middle of the afternoon lunch rush, and there was a steady stream of customers in and out its doors. The smell of roast chicken and fresh baking permeated the air, along with the rich aroma of coffee. Outside, the sun shone brightly with a few clouds hovering in the sky. Remains from the snowstorm two days ago hung around in heaps of white in parking lots and uncleared pathways. The daily temperature was too low to melt it away.

Megan's shift had begun two hours ago; and already, her feet were aching. It would be a double shift today to make up for the one she'd missed a few days ago when Mia had called frantically from the hospital. That and the fact that a lack of sleep contributed to her overall tiredness. It had taken her hours to fall sleep after Noah had left.

"So I hear Noah was at your place last night," Sarah said.

Megan's hands froze for a moment and then continued handing out eating utensils to the ladies.

"Where did you hear that?"

Sarah smiled. "Oh, I have my ways. Just kidding, I overheard Michael and Aaron talking about it this morning. So you want to fill in the rest?"

All three sets of eyes were focused on her, and she found herself feeling uncomfortable by the attention. True, the Thomas family were as thick as thieves, but did they really need to discuss everything with each other? Shifting from one foot to the other, she decided to just answer the question.

"Yeah, he invited himself for a dinner and a movie at my place."

Sarah's eyes narrowed slightly. "Invited himself?"

Megan shrugged. When Noah had first arrived on her doorstep, she had thought it a little strange; but then again, her and Noah's relationship seemed to be built on all things strange.

"Yes, he arrived at my place, ordered dinner, and we watched a movie."

They didn't need to know about the sparks that had bounced between them for the duration of the visit or how many times she'd wondered about what it would be like for Noah to take her into his arms and kiss her. Or how hard she'd tried to ignore the way his attention was focused on her instead of the movie, thrilling her to the point that she was sure her heartbeat could be heard in the four corners of the earth. What would they think of him asking her to dinner? She could only imagine the repercussions of them knowing that.

"What?" she asked.

Sarah smiled, but Dakota answered, "You know, Noah doesn't go out at all—at least, he hasn't in the six months he's been back in town. All he does is work, go to rehab, and mope around his apartment. I think this is the first time he's gone out somewhere we didn't have to drag him kicking and screaming." Dakota's smile widened. "You wouldn't happen to know why, would you?"

Did they think . . . she didn't want to think what. "Uh . . . I don't . . . "

"Leave the girl alone," Lana said, waving her hand to dismiss the discussion. "I, for one, am glad he was out with you. Some company would do that man the world of good after what he's been through. With his parents still in Denver, he needs all the friends he can get."

Megan wondered just how much Lana knew about Noah's past; clearly, it was enough to know that he had one and that it wasn't pretty. Her heart ached, and she smiled, thinking of the times of vulnerability she'd witnessed while with him.

"Megan, table two is seated." Natalie came over, handing Megan two more menus and Lana's pie. And that was her cue to get moving on to the other customers.

"Ladies, if you need anything else, just let me know; and I will be back in a while to check on you." Megan handed Lana her pie and, with a bright smile, moved onto her next table of customers, thankful to be done with the awkward discussion. When she was alone, her mind was already so filled with Noah that she couldn't afford to have him on her mind at work, too.

It was lucky that things at the coffee shop were so busy; more and more of the townspeople were going on vacation, and there were activities planned for the coming weeks before Christmas. In her short time in Snowy Springs, Megan had learned that Christmas was a holiday celebrated for months on end in this small town. It was the biggest tourist attraction of the year; and they did it in style—tree lightings, town parades, a Christmas fair at the community center, and the Christmas pageant on Christmas Eve.

In spite of all the hustle and bustle going on around her, Megan's thoughts kept centering on the night before. The discussion with Sarah and Dakota only added to her confusion. Last night was one of the best nights she'd had in a very long time; and in a large part, that was thanks to Noah. Who could have known that a brutish, angry man could be so kind and caring or that hands that were more prone to weapons and combat could rock a small child to sleep again? The evening had ended with Noah placing a sleeping Isaiah back in her arms, tapping her gently on the nose, and abruptly taking his leave. There had been something in his eyes—a something that she was sure she recognized in herself. It was there in those blue eyes, a tenderness that caused her breath to catch in her chest, a look that made all thought leave her and heated her blood from her face to her toes.

"Megan," Natalie whispered in her ear, bringing her back to her surroundings. "Are you okay?"

"Yes, I am . . . just a lot going on."

"You better get to table two. Grace is watching you."

Megan's gaze came back into focus, seeing Grace at the cash register, her eyebrow raised in question. "Sorry," she mouthed to Grace as she dodged Stacey, one of the other servers, en route to her table. Stacey gave her a sour look, muttering something about Grace's favorite while moving out of Megan's way. Whatever—Megan didn't have time to worry about Stacey and her attitude today.

The rest of her shift rushed by; and when the old cuckoo clock announced it was eight, Megan breathed in a relieved sigh. Her feet ached, and the night was far from over. The paper that should have been in two days ago was still unsubmitted. The weight of it hungover her head. She'd set aside last night to relook at it and submit it; however, the arrival of Noah had blown those plans right out of the water. And when he'd left her, she couldn't seem to focus on anything else besides him.

She sighed again. *Focus, Megan.* She needed to stop thinking of Noah Thomas.

"Megan," Grace called. "Can I see you in my office for a moment?"

Rising, Megan followed Grace past the cash register and into the back office. Grace turned and closed the door firmly behind Megan.

"Yes, Grace."

"It has come to my notice that you have been missing or tardy for shifts on a regular basis."

"Sorry, I know I spoke to you about my last shift; it really was an unavoidable family emergency."

Grace shifted some papers around on her desk, leafing through a pile. "I know you are going through a lot, Megan. And I know that a cancer diagnosis is difficult on a family. I do understand. However, I also am running a business, and I need you to be at your shifts especially during the Christmas rush." Grace smiled, taking some of the heat from her words. Megan's shoulders sagged in relief; she wouldn't be fired today.

"I understand, Grace, and thank you."

"You're welcome. Leave your apron in your locker, and I will see you in the morning for the early shift. Get some rest, Megan; you look like you need it."

Removing her apron and notepad from her pocket, Megan pulled out her messenger bag that acted like a purse and placed her work things back in her locker. She'd been counting on the afternoon shift tomorrow with the hopes of finishing her paper and then sleeping until ten before going to the hospital. But it would be the early shift; she would have to use tonight wisely—and she thought bemusedly, inhale an obscene amount of coffee.

Leaving her thoughts of school and Noah alone for once, another thought took her attention as she swiped open the message on her phone from Mia. Mr. Ambrose would not receive another treatment for a week, and Mia and Tyreke were taking shifts looking after Isaiah and being at the hospital with Mrs. Ambrose. She wished she could offer to help; but the extension on her paper was almost up, and she needed to submit it as soon as possible.

The journey back to her apartment was windy, blowing her woolen scarf into her face and striving to rip her messenger bag from around her body. A frosty, snow-ladened gale blew down the street, cutting through her clothes as she navigated the sizeable icy puddles spread on the concrete sidewalk. Why hadn't she thought to drive her car to work earlier, knowing that by the time she was done, it would be dark?

She stepped over another frozen pool only to lose her balance and land with a hard thump on her butt. *Very smart, Megan; you should have listened to your senses.* Thankfully, she still held a death grip on her messenger bag strap slung onto her shoulder. Carefully pushing herself to standing, she grabbed onto the back of a nearby bench stabilizing her balance. Her hip ached, and she was sure she would have a bruise come tomorrow.

The wind continued to howl, bringing with it a dusting of iced rain and snow. Lamenting again the fact that she should have driven to work earlier, Megan tried to hurry, aching and cold, toward her apartment. The steady frozen drizzle added to the already thick layer of ice on the ground. Megan stepped around a splash of black ice, only to find her feet slipping out from under her again. Arms wheeling, she felt herself going down as pain flared in her left leg. She reached for the bench again to brace herself but was too late. The nasty gust of wind whipped her scarf over her eyes; and she lost her grip on her bag, landing for a second time on the hard ground. The messenger bag slid away from her, its contents spilled out on the ice-covered ground. Megan pushed to her feet a second time reaching for her fallen notebook. She breathed a sign of relief when a familiar truck pulled up to curb and came to a stop.

Chapter Sixteen

"Admit it. You're bad at this, and you know it," Michael said, laughing.

Noah lunged forward for the football, tackling Michael low in the waist. They crashed to the ground with a loud thud. The collision with Michael winded him, but he didn't let that stop him. Still straining to find his breath, Noah leaped to his feet, surprised at how agile he had become since his last therapy session, and pried the small spherical ball from his brother's hands before Michael could mount any resistance. He ran down the astroturf field, ramming the ball down past the goal line.

"Touchdown! Beat that!" He laughed, breath heaving from his lungs. Little by little, his former fitness and strength were returning to his body. Even though he was well past his twenties, he still had what it took to be a good soldier if not for his prosthetic limb. Pushing aside the depressing thoughts that would steal his good mood, Noah collected the ball and ambled back to Michael's side, shoving the ball into Michael's unprotected chest.

"You were saying?" he asked, giving Michael a hand up from the ground.

"I'll admit you're pretty spry for an old man, but you're still bad at throwing."

"Okay, show me then, oh wise one, how it's done." Noah tossed the ball back to Michael and crossed his arms over his chest, waiting.

"It's all in the wrist." Michael spun the football a few times in his hands before raising it shoulder-height and hefting it neatly over the crossbar of the goal post. "See? Easy."

"You two done comparing sport prowess for geriatrics?" Aaron teased as he tossed the ball back to Michael. He rubbed his damp hair with a towel and turned off the alarm blaring from his phone. "I think our time is up. Besides, I have a beautiful lady waiting for me with dinner."

Noah glanced at the clock hanging over the indoor arena: 8:00 p.m. He grabbed his water bottle, downing half the bottle in one long pull, then looked at his brother. Michael was downing his bottle of water while packing up his stuff. Because of the work Michael and Aaron had done last winter on the community center, the mayor allowed them to use the indoor football facilities two nights a week. Usually, there were more guys; but with Christmas less than a month away, many of their team members were busy with work or family commitments. Tonight, only Michael, Aaron, and he could make their weekly game of flag football.

"Right with you. Sarah is making mac and cheese and Lana's coffee cake for dessert." Michael rubbed his flat stomach appreciatively.

Noah snorted, shaking his head. "You two are such saps, you know that?"

"Jealous?" Michael challenged.

It stunned Noah to find that he was, but he wouldn't tell Michael that. "No, thanks. Took that ride on the merry-go-round and not in a hurry for a second."

It was Michael's turn to snort. "That's not what I think. I think you are more ready to move on than you know. It's just a matter of time."

The confidence in Michael's voice stunned Noah. Did his brother know something he didn't? What made him so sure? His thoughts leaped to Megan. How could Michael know that Noah thought of her almost constantly, that when he wasn't otherwise distracted by life, he was thinking about the next opportunity he'd have to intrude on her life? Besides, she had promised to go to dinner with him.

He played it cool, giving nothing away. "What are you going on about?"

Michael glanced at Aaron, an eyebrow raised. "What do you think?"

"More than he knows, poor sap," Aaron answered.

They locked up the room and made their way to the reception desk of the community center to return the key. Aaron waved goodbye and then hurried out into the night, eager for his date with Dakota, Noah presumed.

"Can I talk to you for a minute?" Noah asked Michael.

"Sure."

Together, they walked over to the coffee bar beside the entrance of the community center, got two coffees, and sat down at a nearby table.

"What's on your mind?" Michael asked.

Noah wasn't quite sure how to ask about the thoughts going through his mind. "When you came back, did you ever feel guilty about being the only one in your squad to return?"

Michael took a drink of his coffee, assessing his brother. "Sure, I did. Survivor's guilt—that's what the doc called it. It felt wrong to come back to live a good life when many didn't have that opportunity. Why do you ask?"

"I guess . . . " How did he describe the confusing mix of emotions he felt? "How did you deal with the flashbacks? And the knowledge that others are dead, and you are not?"

"I prayed and remembered to be grateful. It took a while to accept that there was nothing I could have done to save my squad, no matter what I did," Michael replied thoughtfully. "Where are you going with this?"

"I could have done something—stayed away and accepted her choices."

"Noah, you can't keep—"

Noah grimaced and shook his head slightly. "Teneal's death was my fault, even if I wasn't the one driving the other car." It was a heavy burden, one he carried because his guilt would not allow him to lay it down.

"It wasn't your fault, Noah."

He'd heard the words before; and like before, he didn't listen. "I should carry the guilt that I do over it. But recently, it's like . . . " His gaze trailed down to his twisted hands as he squeezed them together and abruptly pulled them apart.

"Hmmm," Michael said, his worried frown bending into a knowing smile. "Like there is sunlight pushing through the dark cloud that has hung over your life. Like the weight of that guilt is getting lighter."

Noah nodded, rubbing his chin. "How can it be? On the one hand, it bothers me—the guilt chews me up inside. And on the other . . . " He sighed. "I don't know."

"Have you prayed about it?"

"You know I left God behind when I joined the army."

"So did I. For the years I was in the desert, I didn't believe that God was active in my life or that He cared one way or another about me." Michael leaned back in his seat and took another drink of his coffee. "I was wrong. I guess you have a choice before you; either you can believe that God still has good for you, or you can let the guilt that sits on your chest continue to squash any chance of happiness you might find."

"I wasn't referring to God, you know. I was trying to find out what to do about Megan."

Michael's smile grew wide. "I know; but sometimes, we need to deal with underlying problems before we deal with heart problems. When I came back to Snowy Springs, I tried hard to find happiness without God and ended making a huge mess of things. I almost lost Sarah in the process. What about you, bro? What are you going to choose?"

Noah had no answer for his brother, only a tempest in his chest and too many "what ifs" to count.

Quietly, they collected their cups and tossed them into the nearby trash bin.

As they made their way through doors into the windy evening, Michael turned to him. "I will continue to pray for you. Don't let the past crush any chance of happiness you have. Make the right choice so that you have no regrets." He clapped him on the shoulder and gave it a quick squeeze. "Night, Noah."

"Night, send love to Sarah."

The roads were less busy than expected as Noah headed in the direction of his apartment. There was one last turn before his road when he spotted a person frantically trying to gather their belongings while the wind did its best to wrest the things from them. Noah pulled over to the curb opposite the bent-down figure and rushed across the ice-strewn road. He was grateful that his footing held once he'd reached the other side. He gripped the notebook as it rolled past him, his hand landing the same time as a small, cold, mittened hand landed above his.

"I got it," he said lifting the notebook. It was soaked from the snow and ice, its pages bent in all directions. Neat print handwriting littered the pages. His head came up and met the beautiful brown eyes that haunted his waking hours. They stared back at him, the relief in their depths obvious.

"Thank you," Megan said. She took the proffered notebook and pushed unsteadily to her feet. In her one hand was a woolen scarf and, in the other, a black leather messenger bag.

"I'm beginning to think you get into these situations on purpose just so I can rescue you," he said, smiling broadly at her.

Red color rushed into Megan's cheeks. "Don't flatter yourself. I was doing just fine. I reached it the same time you did." There was no heat in her words, just a friendly banter.

"Luckily, I don't need my ego stroked." He chuckled.

A small smile bent Megan's mouth. "Luckily."

"What are you doing out in this weather? Did you get another flat?" Noah asked, curling his arm around Megan's back. He guided her toward his truck, trying as best as he could to ignore her scent and the way her body fit to his. It warmed his blood more than two hours with Michael and Aaron on the football field ever did. Megan shivered and then groaned quietly.

"Are you hurt?"

"Just my pride and my hip. I should have listened when the weather app said there would be ice tonight and drove to work."

That would explain the grimace. "Do you need to go to the hospital?"

"Nah, I don't think there is anything a warm bath and sleep couldn't cure."

"Okay."

He opened the passenger door and helped Megan into the seat. The heat was already blowing. Megan lifted her hands to the heating vents, removing her mittens and flexing fingers in the warm air. She sighed appreciatively; and he stalled, watching her movements again before climbing in himself.

Concentrate on the road, the weather, anything but the woman beside you. What kind of ludicrous coincidence allowed his path and Megan's to cross again tonight? Why was it that when he drew to the conclusion that she was better off away from him, she suddenly appeared again in his life? What was more, he welcomed the intrusion like a man starving.

"Better?"

"Thanks," she said quietly. "I was sure I was going to get hyperthermia before I managed to get home."

Worry pierced him, and he pushed it aside. Megan was a grown woman who could look after herself, although sometimes it seemed like she was so busy caring for others that she forgot about herself. "I guess I don't need to tell you how dangerous it is to be out in the cold like that."

"I know. My work isn't far from my apartment, and I thought the walk would do me good after being indoors all day."

"Maybe choose a day where the weather isn't so bad in the future," he said, hating the condescension in his words. As her friend, he hoped she took his words the way they were meant—that he cared about her well-being and wanted her to be safe—more so than a friend.

She nodded wearily. "I will." She leaned her head back against the head rest and closed her eyes. A moment later, the rhythmic movement of her chest slowed to an even pace. She must be exhausted for her to fall asleep with such ease in the condition she was in. He drew the messenger bag gently from Megan's hands and searched for her keys. Finding nothing and not sure what to do but hesitant to wake her, Noah turned his truck around and headed toward his place.

Chapter Seventeen

"Megan," a voice called, "I think you better wake up. It's getting late."

Megan blinked several times as her surroundings came into view. A large stone fireplace popped and rustled as flames danced across the wooden logs. Underneath her, she could feel the rough material of a sofa. The cushions were firm like the sofa had not seen much use. A large red and black checkered blanket lay over her knees, and she saw the toe of her boots sticking out beside the fire. Her black coat, messenger bag, scarf, and notebook lay directly in front of the fire, the heat drying them. A soft groan escaped her as she moved, pain running from her hip down her leg, and she stilled.

Before her gaze could travel further around the room, he spoke again. "Megan."

This time, she turned to the voice. Noah's face was bent with concern, watching her as her brain caught up with her surroundings. He was so handsome. *Really, Megan?*

"How are you feeling?" he asked, crossing the room chair to her. He stopped and frowned and then slid his hands into his front pockets.

"Sore. Where are we?"

"At my place. Sorry, I couldn't find your keys, so I brought you here. I hope you don't mind."

"I don't mind." In fact, as she looked around, the room screamed rugged and Noah. It was furnished with wooden furniture, muted browns, burgundy, and deep blues. At the back of the room, she spied a hallway likely leading to his bedroom. Her gaze followed the dark wood-paneled floor until one room just off the living room had the light still on.

"The kitchen," Noah said, noticing her perusal.

"It's nice. Cozy." And it was. Although the room was rustic, it made her feel warm and like she belonged. *Where had that thought come from?* She turned to Noah again to meet his smirk.

"I'd offer to give you the tour, but I think you have had enough for one night."

She shifted, the pain in her hip springing to life again. "Yeah, I think you might be right. I am gonna feel this hip in the morning." A clock ticked over somewhere in the room, and she glanced at it: 11:00 p.m. "Well, maybe in a few hours," she mused.

"I think you need to eat something. Am I right in saying you haven't had dinner?"

Megan's head bent to look at her hands. How did he know? "Too busy." When was the last time she had eaten? Lunch time. There had been that one small piece of pie she'd shared with Natalie between shifts. That counted, didn't it?

"That's what I thought. Luckily, I can help with that."

Circling her to a table set up behind them, Noah retrieved two bowls from the tabletop and made his way over to the sofa. She shifted to face forward and gladly took the bowl as he offered it to her. It smelled warm, familiar, and like a welcoming hug. She sniffed appreciatively, and her stomach growled in anticipation.

"It's Sarah's chicken soup. Just the thing for a cold night like this one," Noah said with a small laugh.

Megan brought the soup to her lips and took a drink, its heat instantly radiating down her throat into her chest, warming her. "How long have I been out?" she asked.

"Two hours or so. When was the last time you got a good night's sleep?"

Megan shrugged, "I don't know. Between work, school, and the family, I haven't really been getting a lot. I guess I just crashed. Sorry you had to be the one to rescue me *again.*"

Noah shoulders rose up and then sagged down. "I don't mind. I am glad you're okay. Tonight could have ended a lot worse than it did."

That was true. Cold weather and exhaustion did not make a good pairing, and either one could have cost her life.

Megan suddenly startled, nearly dropping her bowl. "I was supposed to submit my paper tonight." She placed the bowl unsteadily on the table beside her, pushing aside the warmth of the blanket and reaching for her messenger bag. Everything was still inside. Next, she checked her notebook. Her notes were a little smudged for their encounter with the snow; but otherwise, she could still read them. When she got home, it would be a short procedure to get her paper done. Noah ate quietly as she placed her things back by the fire.

"Megan, why don't you finish up that soup, and then I will take you home?"

Megan sat down, anxiety rippling through her chest. Quiet descended between them. It was a comfortable silence, as each one ran through their own thoughts. Her thoughts moved far away from her paper, landing on the way the firelight rippled over Noah's rugged features, the light of the flames brushing lines of bronze and brown over his hair. He stared straight ahead, his features carved out in bold, attractive lines. Was she checking Noah out? Yes, she totally was.

Why did they keep running into each other? It was like every time she needed someone, he appeared: the day at the hospital, the night when she desperately needed some company, and now, when she might have frozen to death because of her lack of concentration. She might have once believed in coincidence, but not so with them. As crazy as it sounded in her head, it was like there was some Force out there bringing them together again and again. But for what purpose? What would it serve for them to be in each other lives?

Unable to find answers to her questions, she picked up the bowl of soup and emptied the contents, placing it once again on the table. As promised, it was delicious and hopefully would give her enough energy to still put her outstanding paper behind her when she eventually got home.

"Thank you. That was delicious," she said.

"You're welcome."

Noah emptied his bowl, placed it on the coffee table, and then leaned back into the sofa, sighing softly. His one arm stretched along the back, close enough that she could feel the heat of his skin against her shoulder. Or maybe she was only imagining it. Had she always been so aware of this man? Warmth fluttered in the pit of her stomach, moving with a languid motion into her chest. Small sparks ignited where his leg accidentally brushed hers as he moved his hand through his hair. And then he turned to look at her.

The rhythmic pulse of her heart sped to double time as his gaze held hers. His blue eyes darkened and softened, drawing her deeper into a whirlpool of unknown emotion. Hesitantly, he reached out and took her hand; slowly, as if studying her skin, he ran his finger one by one up and down each of hers. She shivered as he swirled the pad of his forefinger at the center of her palm before moving to the other hand. The feelings moving through her were so unfamiliar that she wasn't sure whether she should ask him to stop or tell him to go on. It wasn't as if she had never been attracted to a man before nor been in a relationship; but somehow, this was different, more intense and therefore far more alarming.

His gaze burned her. She felt something inside her answering the hunger she saw churning in those stormy blue depths, a craving to decrease the space between them if only so she could be closer to that heat. Megan swallowed hard, staying the impulse. This level of intensity could only lead down one path, a path she wasn't sure she was willing to take. Noah had been married before and was experienced in the matters of the heart and body. What would he expect of her if she allowed herself to indulge in the attraction between them?

"Noah, I . . . "

"Megan," Noah said. His voice was deep and husky, the tenor sending another pleasant wave of heat up her spine. He knitted his fingers between hers, sighed, and then let her go, moving as far as the sofa would allow. "I think I should take you home."

"Yes," she said breathlessly. "I think that would be a good idea."

Without another word, Noah stood and handed Megan her shoes. He held her coat for her as she slipped it on, pausing for a moment to hug her close from behind as he tucked the coat around her. His slight intake of breath as he stepped back told her it was not an accident. She found that she didn't mind. She wanted to be held by him as much as his actions told her he wanted to hold her.

Turning to face him and aware of the electricity fanning the air between them, she could not allow herself even that small desire. He seemed to understand and grinned at her.

"Why don't you get the rest of your stuff while I warm up the truck?"

He turned on his heel; pulled on his boots; and, without his jacket or hat, walked into the dark, cold night.

Megan felt the loss of his presence, although her body still hummed and her heart still beat out a loud rhythm. She took a deep breath and another to calm herself. What would it help? She would just have to do it again as soon as she joined him in the car. How could she let this happen, she thought as she moved around Noah's living room. It smelled like him; everything she touched and each time she inhaled his woodsy scent burned into her senses. She filled her arms with her belongings and made her way to where Noah waited.

Trying to be friends with Noah when the attraction between them was so strong would be an effort in futility. So what? What would she do about it? Allow him in? She had already done that to a certain extent. Noah knew more about her than most, and he was becoming more and more a part of her life each day. Would she allow them to become more? Noah wanted to be more. He held himself back; she could see it. Would she be the brave one and cross that divide, or would she continue to resist and hope against hope that it would go away?

"Would you like to go out tomorrow night?" Noah asked once they were on the road back to her apartment.

"As friends?" she asked.

Noah stared at her a long time before answering, "If you'd like." Something flitted across his expression like he was debating something with himself. He roughly cleared his throat. "I would like to take you out on a date."

There, he'd made his intentions clear. The only thing stopping them from taking the step forward was a word from her. Was she prepared for what that word would mean for them?

"Like a date, date?" she asked.

Noah smiled, inclining his head to her, a smile that told her he was onto her. "I think after what almost just happened back there, it would probably be better if I took you on a date first."

Heat filled her cheeks as she nodded. "That would probably be wiser." She curled her fingers into each other, startled when their movement was stopped by one of his hands covering hers.

"Noah you've been married before," she said. Her face was so hot, and she wasn't sure if she could get to the point of what she was trying to say.

"Yes." He seemed confused. "Does that bother you?"

"No, but I have to ask . . . " Her hands fidgeted under his, and he stilled them with a gentle squeeze. She felt his stare and looked up. His expression lightened, and he smiled gently, kindly. With it, she knew he understood where she was going.

"Megan, I value the commitments of marriage and would never ask you to do anything that would make you uncomfortable." He brought up one of her hands, brushing his mouth against her skin. There went her heart again. "I would really love to go out with you. Let's start there."

There it was, and now it was her turn.

"In that case, I would love to."

Chapter Eighteen

"Noah, you in here?" Michael called, stamping his feet on the rough mat at the entrance of the barn.

Noah stared at the stack of trees in need of baling, lost in thought. As much as he tried, he couldn't seem to bring his concentration under control and with it the anxiety that somehow, he had made a terrible decision. Megan had said yes to a date, and here he was unsure of whether asking her had been the right thing to do in the first place. Everything inside him had wanted to kiss her last night; he'd dreamed of kissing her, waking up and forcing himself outside to cool down. He'd thought of nothing else in the intervening hours since he'd dropped her off at her apartment. The temptation had almost overcome him then, too.

He pushed his hand through his hair, clearing his mind of the dream. Last night, as he sat with the blanket on the sofa still covered in her scent, he'd made the decision to be honest with himself. When he had first laid eyes on Megan Davis, he'd immediately been attracted to her; however, in the short time he'd known her, that attraction had changed into something warm, tender, and wholly unwelcome—at least, that was what he'd thought. He'd changed his mind, and so, it seemed, had his heart. They were both vested in her now. Megan cared too much for those she loved, to the extent that it had cost her sleep, peace of mind, nutrition, and even time to complete those things she desperately needed to do, like her unsubmitted assignment. She was kind, funny, and yet mature enough to put someone like him in his place.

"Yeah, in the back."

Alarm crossed Michael's face as he saw Noah, his foot balanced on a barrel, hat in his hand, arms crossed over his knee, staring at nothing. If Michael could read his thoughts, he might disagree, but all Noah could see was the ways that he would mess up. Flashes of the night Teneal had died flickered the corners of his memory, and he blinked them away.

"What happened?" Michael asked, crossing his arms over his chest, his frown meeting the bridge of his nose.

"I asked Megan out," Noah said, unable to keep the disbelieving sadness out of his voice.

Michael's eyebrows brushed his forehead and then once again dipped into a frown. "And? There must be more to it for you to look like you lost your favorite weapon."

A grin he couldn't hold back slid over his face, and Noah turned to his brother, "It's worse than that."

"What could be worse than that?"

"She said yes." Amazing as it was.

"And? Shouldn't you be happy or at least a little excited?"

"I am . . . " Michael would laugh his pants off when he heard of what a wuss his no-nonsense, no-time-for-weakness brother was about to say. "What if I mess up?"

Compassion filled his brother's eyes; and Michael walked over to clasp Noah's arm, squeezing it gently. "After our discussion yesterday, I was almost sure you were going to walk away from Megan. I thought maybe you would convince yourself that anything that could happen there was a bad idea. What changed?"

Feeling a bit like a teenager caught in his first crush, Noah's cheeks turned ruddy "Last night, after we left the community center, I ran into Megan. She was in a bind. I ended up taking her back to my place, made her dinner, and took her home." He sighed, remembering the way he had almost lost his head and thankful for Whatever was out there that he'd had the strength to walk away. Megan lit him up like no other, and he was unsure how long he could continue to fight his attraction.

His thoughts must've been written over his face because Michael chuckled. "Did you kiss her?"

"How did you . . . " He couldn't stop the words before they ran from his mouth. Clenching his jaw, he said through his teeth, "No." And did he regret it. "Not that I didn't have the opportunity or the inclination."

"What stopped you?"

"Teneal. The past. A desperate need to not screw things up. Who knows?" He clenched his hand into a fist and then released the tension. "Thankfully, I held onto sense long enough to not follow through. I wanted to. Man, did I want to."

He didn't like the understanding he saw on Michael's face or the compassion still burning in his eyes. If Noah thought back to his brother's own journey to love, the position he had put himself in, his hesitancy and reluctance and his desire to do the right thing were all things Michael understood.

"Did this happen before or after you asked her out?"

"Before."

"And you still asked her out?"

What had he been thinking? He nodded, planting both feet on the ground. He pushed his hat onto his head and his hands into the side pockets of his corduroy jacket.

"I have to say, Noah, I'm really confused."

"That makes two of us."

"Do you like her?"

"Yes."

"And you want to go out with her?"

"Yes."

"So what's stopping you? Really stopping you? If you had to write a list of reasons you and Megan shouldn't be together, what would your reasons be?" Michael expression softened, a half-smile lifting his lips. "When I left Sarah and moved back to Denver, I thought I was doing the right thing for Sarah. I had a list of reasons—my PTSD, Lucas, my fears, my lack of faith, the ugliness of what I had experienced—whatever I could think of. At the end of the day, those were good reasons but not insurmountable reasons. Once I made my peace with God, many of those reasons disappeared; and I could be the man I thought Sarah needed. Turns out, it was the man I needed to be, too."

Noah allowed himself to sag down onto a nearby bench and dropped his head into his hands. Why was this so complicated? *Teneal,* he thought. His ability to make decisions had significantly been impacted by his and Teneal's relationship and the evening that had ended her life.

Michael sat down beside him. "What are your reasons, Noah, and are they truly as insurmountable as you think?" He clapped Noah on the shoulder and stood, leaving him with his thoughts.

Noah stood and started up the tree baler, moving with practiced ease. He had gone through the process of baling trees so often in the week he had worked for Buck that it was almost second nature.

Michael paused at the open door. "I have an idea. We are having a carol's evening at the church on Saturday. Invite Megan. See how it goes," Michael said. "Maybe then, things will become clearer for you."

Noah grunted in response and said no more. Michael sighed, leaving Noah with his dark thoughts.

As the trees were thinned, sanitized, and baled, Noah mulled over Michael's words. He wrote a list in his head of why being with Megan would be good or if he was leading himself and Megan into a monumental disaster. By the time the last of the twenty or so trees had passed into the machine, Noah was sure he had decided what he could live with. He and Megan had not agreed on a day to go out, and in that could be an answer. However, he wasn't a coward. He would do right by Megan and tell her before it was too late.

The sun had sunk below the horizon, and snow once again fell in splendid patterns from the gray sky. Noah slapped his icy gloves against the barn door and closed it for the night, sliding the lock into place. The ground crunched as he walked over it, forming shoe-sized patterns in the mounting white powder. He stopped and stared out into the vista around him, his mind still mulling over the plans he had tonight—plans he hoped would bring him the closure he so desperately needed.

For the first time since he'd left the hospital, he was going to visit Teneal. His truck door creaked as he opened it, the hinges whining against the rapidly dropping temperatures. As he turned the ignition, the truck rumbled to life, bringing with it the blast of cold air. He shivered as the air slowly warmed, and he slid the gear shift into drive.

Fort Logan National Cemetery was a two-hour drive from Snowy Springs. The distance gave him the time to gather his thoughts and reasons why he was making the trip. It was to say goodbye. He didn't know if he was ready to let go; but if anything was going to happen between him and Megan, he had to put Teneal and their relationship where it belonged—in the past.

When Teneal had walked out, something in him had died. He'd been too stubborn, too busy, and too angry to deal with that something. Instead, he'd held his anger like a shield protecting himself from feeling, from living. He sighed and rubbed his leg as a phantom pain shot through the lower part. The body always remembered. Where had he heard that before?

Pressing the gas pedal, the truck lurched forward along the dark highway stretched out like a black sentinel watching him as he covered the miles. He drove on.

The sky was completely dark by the time he pulled to a stop outside the gates covered by the afternoon's snow fall. Skeletal trees hung over the white gravestones; their spindly branches bore remains of the earlier storm. A blue and white sign hung above the enormous bronze lock: closed for the evening. It was probably for the best. He'd made it this far. He could wait until the next morning to see her.

He leaned his head against the rest behind and allowed himself to relive the night moment by moment, watching himself as he found the note, then made the decision to go after Teneal, even though the weather forecast was bad. He remembered the surprise on Teneal's face when he'd pulled up to her apartment building in Pleasant Valley and demanded she come with him. Why had she agreed? Had she known he would insist until she folded?

The drive back to their place in Glen Eagle—he released a shuddering breath as the accident followed. Those memories were startlingly clear, like someone had filmed them in 4K high definition and burned them into his brain. The sound of screeching tires pierced his ears. He shuddered, covering them with his hands. Air rushed from his body as the impact came, and then there was only darkness.

Noah shook himself out of the reverie, gasping. One droplet rolled down his cheek, followed by another and another until he was rasping for air, unable to stop the torrent of his sorrow flowing down his face. Pain from remembered bruising exploded from his body, and the phantom pains in his leg from earlier burst into flame until he thought he would scream from the agony. Why had he been so stupid?

He knew. He'd loved her. Her leaving had hurt so bad, he thought he would split apart from the pain. He hadn't known how to let her go. Emotion continued to pound him until, at last, the tempest settled. *I'm sorry, Teneal.*

Noah blinked, wiping away the remaining tears with the back of his hand. He pressed his head more firmly into the headrest, drawing deep, steadying breaths in through his nose and out his mouth until the tight pain in his chest eased. *I'm so very sorry. Please forgive me.*

Just then, he noticed someone watching him from the gate of the cemetery. An old man, perhaps the caretaker, walked up to the truck and waved for Noah to open the window. Noah obliged.

"Can I help you, young man?" he asked.

Noah swallowed hard and nodded. "I've got someone I need to see." His voice was hoarse after his tears.

"You know the cemetery closes after sundown."

"Yes."

The man watched Noah for a long time, assessing. "I can give you twenty minutes, and then I need to lock the gates."

It would be long enough to say goodbye. "Thank you."

Chapter Nineteen

"Megan, what a lovely surprise," Mr. Ambrose said and tried weakly to sit up in his hospital bed. His once-robust brown cheeks held a grayish tinge, and his eyes were tired. His smile was the same when he saw her—wide and welcoming.

Moving gingerly, he opened his arms to her; and her own need to be held moved her into his embrace. His hug was warm and enveloped her like it had from the first time he had met her more than five years ago. The room smelled like antiseptic and sickness. The smell turned her stomach; but with her face buried in Mr. Ambrose's chest, he would be unable to see her expression.

"How are you?" she asked as he released her from the embrace. She hooked a chair behind her with her hand and pulled it closer to the hospital bed, seating herself.

"Oh, I feel better."

"Is there anything I can get you?" Megan asked. A convoluted mix of emotions Megan struggled with filled her chest: love for this dear man who had been there for her, the sadness that made his presence necessary, and the knowledge that he would soon be leaving her. Megan wished she could let go of her loyalty to her own parents and embrace the fatherly relationship Mr. Ambrose offered. How could she replace that loyalty and affection with this new one? Tyreke often said that allowing Mr. Ambrose to be a fatherly figure to her was not exchanging one for the other, merely embracing a widening circle. She'd struggled with her thoughts and feelings, not able to make the distinction.

The room descended into silence. Megan shifted awkwardly in her seat.

Seeming to sense her unease, Mr. Ambrose smiled. "No, thank you. What brings you here tonight?"

"Mia said the doctors said the treatment wasn't working." Her voice sounded small, childlike even to herself. "I came to see for myself how you were doing."

Surprisingly, Mr. Ambrose chuckled. "What do doctors know?" His smile was soft, and his wide, brown eyes were peaceful. He pushed himself up in the raised hospital bed and settled the white waffle-like blanket over his legs. "It seems the good Lord has chosen eternal means to heal me. And despite what it means, I am okay with that."

She'd known that there was little hope for recovery; but the easy way Mr. Ambrose accepted his passing was unbearable, not to mention how it unnerved her. Wasn't he afraid to die? How did he have such peace when he didn't know what awaited him on the other side, if there even was one?

"But what about Mrs. Ambrose, Mia, Isaiah, Tyreke?" The dismay she felt was voiced in the rushing of her words.

Mr. Ambrose sighed softly, his smile dipping. "I hate to leave them in this world without me, but I know the good Lord will look after them. I am not afraid to die because I know what is waiting for me, and I know the One Who will look after those I leave behind. I can leave with the knowledge that one day, I will see them again."

His words felt sure and peaceful on her ears; and despite her disbelief at them, she knew with 100 percent certainty, Mr. Ambrose believed them to be true. How she longed for a certainty like his.

"How can you be so sure? How do you know what there is after death?" There was an urgency inside her to speak her biggest fears. Among them were losing Tyreke, Mia, and Isaiah; never finishing university; and the biggest one, she was afraid to die. That question kept her up some nights, spreading anxiety like a sickness through her veins.

A soft brown hand covered hers; and she startled. "Megan, since your parents passed, I have considered you and Tyreke as my own children, and I know Amana feels the same. You two are as precious to us as Mia or Isaiah." He cleared his throat and took a swallow from the glass on his bedside table. "I can understand that Tyreke has welcomed us as a part of your family; he needed to for Mia's sake. But you hold yourself back. Now, for whatever reason you do it is your business; however, I want you to know that we are here for you in whatever capacity we can be. We are your family." There was no judgment, only compassion and wisdom in his gaze. Guilt pressed hard into Megan's shoulders.

"What confounds me," he continued, "is that you are always there for everyone, setting aside your own needs to take care of theirs. You hold yourself back. As noble as this trait is, I wish you would let us help you on the odd occasion. Makes us at least feel a little useful." He smiled.

It was always there just over the next hill in the back of her mind. She loved her parents and, up until this moment, thought she was doing a pretty good job of keeping her needs away from where everyone could see them. She'd been wrong to think someone would not eventually notice. Her eyes grew hot, and she blinked hard against their welling.

"What are you so afraid of?" he asked.

"Dying, losing everyone I love . . . " she said.

He nodded slowly. "Death is not something to be feared if you know Jesus. Then the next stage of the journey is clear." His expression softened into a smile. "That is the reason I am not afraid of dying—because I know what lies ahead of me."

"What is it?"

"Not a what but a where and a Who: Heaven, streets of gold, singing angels, and"—he paused, his smile growing—"the moment I will see Jesus face to face."

He reached for the book resting beside him and flipped reverently through the soft pages. They rustled as he pushed them over. Placing the Bible on his lap, he pointed to a passage. "John 11:25: 'Jesus said to her, *I am the resurrection and the life. The one who believes in me will live even though they die.*' For this, I can know that my future in life or in death is secure with Him." He gently took her hands in his again. "What about you, Megan? What does your future hold? Where will eternity take you?"

She didn't have an answer to any of those questions. And yet, there the answers were, right in front of her, a certain path and a clear future waiting for her to believe.

"I will think on what you have said," she said before she stood to make her goodbyes. Turning, she reached for the door and then turned back to Mr. Ambrose. "Thank you for loving Tyreke and me. I hope you know, despite my reticence, you and Mrs. Ambrose are very dear to me." She hugged him again. "Mia has become the sister I always wanted."

At this, Mr. Ambrose laughed. "I wish I would be around to see how much trouble the two of you will get into in the years to come as Isaiah grows."

Megan laughed, saying her goodbyes and then closing the door behind her as she left. Mr. Ambrose had offered her hope this evening, but a choice was before her. Would she continue to struggle, or would she take the answers given to her and believe?

The rest of the evening passed in a blur as she hurried home, rushed dinner down her throat, and finally settled down to submit her very late paper. As she wrote, the words Mr. Ambrose had shared with her came to life. She studied and edited and waxed between topics and layouts of her assignment. Five hours later and copious amounts of coffee, she finally hit the submit button. There, it was done.

Relief as sweet as summer rain fell from her shoulders. She had done it and would still be well on her way to completing this semester's courses as planned. Soon, she would be done and her future secure. Along with these thoughts came Noah and the complicated position they found themselves in. Was she falling in love with the man, or was it just a fleeting wave of attraction—an intense, exciting attraction. She liked him—perhaps *more* than liked him, which sounded so juvenile to her. What was there between like and love? Whatever there was, she knew she was falling for him. The realization should have stunned her. It didn't. When she thought of Noah, there was no other recourse for her but to fall for a man who gave so much, asking little from her in return.

She stood collecting her dishes, quickly cleaning them and the kitchen before turning in. The neat stack of extra baby bottles reminded Megan of the night Noah had been there. Warmth filled her chest, and she wondered again at what she felt for the man. Beside her on the table, her phone beeped with the voicemail tone. She hadn't even heard it ring.

Hi, Megan, I hope you have had a good day. I was wondering if you would like to join me for a pre-date date at Snow Town Coffee tomorrow.

There was a long moment of silence and then a deep sigh.

Tomorrow afternoon, if you're not busy, say lunch time? Okay, this is Noah, by the way. Okay, goodbye.

She giggled at the nervousness that was so obvious in his voice and smiled at the idea of going out with Noah. There was no hesitation as she responded with a quick text message of acceptance to the date and completed cleaning up the aftereffects of assignment submission.

While she got ready for probably the first good night's sleep in over a week, she reminisced about the way he took care of her when she needed him, how he made sure she ate when she'd forgotten to—and then, of course, there was the almost-kiss a couple of nights ago. Her stomach fluttered remembering the intense deepening color of his eyes as his gaze delved into hers, the way her heart had reacted to his nearness thrumming in her chest. Although the night had ended unexpectedly, she was sure if they were ever in that position again, she would find herself thoroughly kissed.

Her face warmed at the thought. And should that happen, she would not complain at all. For the longest time, relationships had not been a priority for her. When Mia and Tyreke had wed, she'd been over-the-moon happy for them; however, she hadn't seen that kind of future for herself. She was focused on her studies and getting her degree, hoping to go on and make a difference in peoples' lives. That had all changed since Noah had entered the picture. Her desires for herself moved from being single to thoughts of what it was like to be part of a couple. Could she see herself as a wife someday? Married to Noah and raising a family? Did Noah want to get married again after the bad experience he had with his first wife? Did she want a family? Did Noah?

Noah would make a wonderful father; that much was clear by the way he interacted with Isaiah. He seemed to naturally know how to calm the infant, how to hold him, and genuinely enjoyed being with him. Megan sighed, shaking her head as she folded Isaiah's blankets and straightened the contents of the pack-and-play. *Way to get ahead of yourself, girl.* It was only a date, and here she was thinking about a future together.

Muttering at the silliness of her thoughts and telling herself to get to bed, Megan changed into her pajamas, turned back the covers, and slid under the comforter. As best she could, she tried to quiet her mind from thoughts of what Mr. Ambrose had said to her competing with her mooning over Noah Thomas. It was still a long time before sleep came.

Chapter Twenty

Noah shifted uneasily, once again sliding his hands into the front pockets of his jeans. An icy wind whistled across the busy street, raising the skin of his uncovered neck. He burrowed deeper into the wool collar of his jacket. Why was he so nervous? It was only coffee. He grimaced. Yes, it was only coffee, but it was coffee with Megan.

Last night, he had taken the step and called her and spent every moment since then questioning whether he had done the right thing. When had he turned into such a wimp?

An unseasonal rumble of thunder grumbled across the rapidly darkening sky. The snow, which had begun as light spirals of white, was now ebbing and flowing with the whistling breeze. He pulled his woolen hat tighter on his head and then, with a sigh, ripped it off, freeing his head to the cold. Maybe it would help clear his worried mind. He chuckled at his own melodrama and crossed the street to Delmonte's Bakery.

As he reached the door, he was met by Lana Bakker. "Good afternoon, Noah," she said cheerfully.

"Afternoon, Lana," he replied, pushing open the door and gesturing for her to go ahead of him. She smiled gratefully, nodding.

"Thank you, I can't seem to stay away from Mary's cinnamon latte. It's just perfect for keeping me warm, and Mary says the cinnamon is excellent for my arthritis." She chuckled.

"How is it feeling today?"

"Oh, much better, thank you. Sarah had a good talk with Jenny at the pharmacy, and we found some kind of cream that helps in this weather."

"I'm glad to hear it helps," he said.

He scanned the room, pushing his hand through his untidy hair, scrunching his hat into his back pocket.

"Are you looking for someone?" Lana asked.

"Yes, but she doesn't seem to be here yet."

Another ominous rumble came from the sky, spiraling his already-apprehensive mood further down. This was a mistake. He should call Megan and cancel. In the mood he was in, his coffee date with Megan was going to be a disaster before it had even started.

"Anyone I know?" Lana asked, drawing his attention back to the diminutive lady before him.

Noah felt his neck heat and cleared his throat. "Just a friend," he replied.

The last thing he wanted was wind of his date with Megan reaching Sarah and Michael; he would never hear the end of it. Just as the thought of calling and canceling came to mind again, a wonderful sight caught his eyes; and he felt a smile bend his lips.

Lana's gaze followed his to where Megan was crossing the threshold of the coffee shop. She smiled up at him, winked, and then made herself to the counter to place her order.

He sighed. By the end of the day, Michael no doubt would know about his date. Oh well, he thought, watching as Megan closed the door behind her, a light dusting of snow covering her hair; it was bound to happen, small town and all. He watched as she handed her coat to a helpful waitress turning her gaze to the busy dining room searching for him. When she found him, she smiled, a beautiful, full, welcoming smile. Air whooshed from his lungs, pushing his pulse into the peak heart rate zone. He blinked, smiling in return, pleased to see warm color rush into her cheeks.

Nerves pressed against the lining of his stomach. He flexed his fingers to stop them, wondering again if he was doing the right thing. Since when had he started sounding like a mushy Christmas card or some such nonsense?

Noah crossed the room to Megan. "Hi," he said, taking one of her arms gently in his hand and drawing her into a hug. Megan sank into the embrace, stirring up the desire to extend the hug. Noah unwound his arms and stepped back, reminding himself they were in public place.

"Why don't we go and find our seats?"

Megan nodded. Her cheeks were flushed, and it gave him untold pleasure to know that she was as affected as him by the embrace.

"Hi," she said, scooting into the booth and setting her purse down on the seat beside her.

"Is here okay?"

She nodded. She looked tired; lightly concealed bags lay under her expressive eyes. They shone with sadness, pain, and ever-present fatigue. Was she as happy to see him as he was to see her?

"Forget your gloves again?" he teased.

Soft color filled her cheeks. "Yes, I think I left them at the hospital again."

He entwined their fingers, giving her plenty of time to pull away should she need to. She didn't. Tenderness for her filled him as he slowly ran his fingertips over the skin of her hand. She shivered, and his heart raced.

"How is he?"

Megan sighed heavily, burdened by the answer. "No better, no worse, I think." She swallowed. "The doctor says the treatment has stalled. The tumors in his lungs aren't getting smaller or fewer." Her voice caught on the last words.

Noah rubbed the pads of his fingers over her knuckles, hoping the small gesture would bring her some comfort.

"I am sorry. Is there no other medicine they can try?"

"Mia says there is an experimental drug they could try. The cost is astronomical, and there is no guarantee it will work." She swallowed, her grip tightening in his. "I don't think that is what Mr. Ambrose wants. I think he is content to die, and I don't blame him. He is so sure of his path forward. He seems at peace with it."

"What do you think they will do?"

"I think in the end, they will accept his decision and let the cancer take its course. The alternative is as horrific as the end result."

Her shoulders slumped. Aware they were in public but caring little for prying eyes, Noah curled his arm around her shoulders and drew her closer to his side. Megan snuggled closer and then sighed in contentment. His heart rioted inside him; and he let it, knowing that this is what she needed from him in this moment.

A waitress appeared at their table. "Hi, my name is Cherie. Can I get you something?"

"Black coffee for me."

"I'll have the same," Megan said.

"Sure, I'll be right back with that." Cherie moved to the next table to take their order.

"Do you usually drink your coffee boring?" he asked, hoping to lighten the heavy cloud over Megan.

The edge of her mouth quirked up. "Boring?"

Noah smiled. "Michael is convinced I should try to make my coffee less 'boring,' as he terms it, by adding milk or flavoring or something like that. But I think, why mess with perfection?"

"I usually enjoy one of those frou-frou type drinks, but I think today demands straight black coffee." The smile dropped from her mouth. "Kinda suits my mood." She paused, eyes wide. "I'm so sorry. I should have said no when you called. I'm not good company today."

Another rumble sounded in among the tumbling snow, and the wind beat the falling flakes into the frosted windows.

"Neither am I," he said wryly. "I hate thunderstorms, even the weird type that come when it is snowing." He released her and rubbed his chin, leaning back into the firm leather at his back. "Reminds me too much of that night with Teneal."

Megan smiled despite her pain, her face framed in compassion. "Tell me about her."

Noah shifted in his seat, suddenly uncomfortable with the direction their conversation had taken. "Are you sure?" he asked, surprised how much her interest in the subject warmed him—not because he was still living in the past but because she wanted to know about him. His mood was still bleak; however, where earlier he'd wanted to cancel their plans, go back to his place, and hide, he found he wanted her company, craved it, even.

"Teneal was . . ." He rubbed his chin searching for the right words. "One of those people who knew everyone and everyone knew. She was vivacious and like a force of nature." He sighed, lost in memories. "Her confidence was one of the first things that drew me to her. She had this fiery red hair and the personality to go with it."

It had been eighteen years since the first time he'd met her. "My buddy Kevin was entranced with Teneal's best friend. We hung out often; and eventually, I gathered up the courage to ask her out." He stared down at the brown-tinted table, remembering. When they'd first met, Teneal had scared the tar out of him, and he was sure she was so far out of his league that he didn't even try. When they had eventually become a couple, it was a running joke between them those early years. "Anyway, we went out on two dates, and the rest is history."

"I'm sorry. It sounds like you two loved each other very much."

"I thought we did. I was so sure until . . ." Did he really want to rehash his past again? Let Megan see what a failure as a husband he had been?

Cherie appeared at the table, two cups of coffee in hand. "Can I get you anything else?"

Noah glanced at Megan, and she subtly shook her head. "Maybe give us a few more minutes?"

"Sure," Cherie said, bustling away to the next table.

"Until?" Megan took a sip of her coffee, grimacing at the taste. He wanted to laugh, but the past held him firm.

"Until she decided the life of a military wife was not what she had signed up for. That was the catalyst that led to the fight. You know the rest."

Megan made a sound of sympathy, her face troubled. "I'm sorry." She gently placed her mug on the tabletop and reached across for his hands. He allowed her to take them and felt comforted by the touch, her skin against his, like a soothing balm to his world-weary soul. Thoughts of kissing her again invaded his mind, not realizing how much those thoughts had overtaken his actions until his face was inches from hers and warm color once again filled her sepia-colored cheeks. *Oops.* Breathing in her intoxicating scent was doing strange things to his control.

He cleared his throat, pressing back a few inches, and dropped his voice low. "Despite everything, I would really like to kiss you right now," he whispered. It wasn't a reaction to his sadness about Teneal. It was Megan—the way her presence soothed him and made him believe things about himself that he had not had the strength to for a long time. She made him believe that maybe he could be enough; maybe, with Megan, he could be the man he wanted to be.

Turning to the side, he leaned closer and kissed a soft press of his lips to her cheek. He suppressed a groan, feeling his control melting. Not good. *Keep your head, Thomas.* He moved a little further away from her, creating space and clearing his ability to think straight.

The color in Megan's cheeks grew more noticeable. "I'm not sure here would be the best place. We have quite an audience, don't you think?" Her voice was breathless.

He had noticed how busy the coffee shop was and was not really inclined to care. Did that mean she wanted him to kiss her?

"And if we didn't have an audience?" he asked, leaning just a little closer to whisper in her ear. A smile swept over his mouth when she shivered.

"Ask me again then," she said. She gently pushed him away, back over to his side of the booth. Noah's insides vibrated with tension. He circled his coffee mug with his hands and drew two deep breaths.

Megan calmly took her second sip of coffee, her face bending into a disgusted expression at the flavor.

"Until then," he said, lifting his own mug to his lips.

Chapter Twenty-One

"Are you warm enough?" Noah asked, gently squeezing Megan's hand as they walked down the well-lit street. They'd spent the last few hours talking about everything and anything until closing time at the coffee shop had come. Snow floated down from the heavens—not enough to coat the ground but short bursts of rushing motion before calming once again to peaceful hovering and flickering between the merry Christmas lights on the sidewalk. The temperature held steady below zero as the night pulled its curtains over the pastel-colored sky. It was so strange how time moved in the winter, long night hours and short days.

Megan didn't mind today, her heart still warm from the discussion with Noah and his confession. A part of her worried about how different she was from his ex-wife. She wasn't vivacious or a redhead; she tended to prefer the company of a small group of good friends than large groups of people. She was younger than Noah, although his assurance that age was just a number did a lot to assuage that worry. But still, why did he want to be with her?

The mention of kissing earlier both thrilled and terrified her. What if as experienced as he was, he found her wanting? Megan had been given her fair share of kisses in high school, but this was different. She'd never wanted to be kissed by someone as much as she did with Noah, nor had she ever seen the obvious attraction a man had for her as she did with Noah. Her gaze lifted to his face; and she took in his profile, softly lit by the streetlights as they walked. How was it that this handsome man, who could probably have any woman, wanted to be with her? Well, most of the time, he did.

There was still a hesitancy in Noah, something that held him back, something she hoped would not end up breaking her heart. Was it the memory of his ex-wife that held him, or was there some other reason? She wished she knew or had the courage to ask. Maybe she would sometime but not tonight. Not when they'd stopped walking and Noah turned her to him.

She lifted her gaze to meet his and shivered in a good way at what she saw there. The normal slate blue in his eyes transformed into a raging tempest of hues and emotions she feared she would drown in. Her pulse sped up, a quiet gasp leaving her otherwise dry throat. This was it, the moment she'd dreamed of since the learning the name Noah Thomas.

Noah reached up, gently brushing off the snowflakes on her nose, leaving a trail of heat wherever he touched. His other arm slid from her hip around to the small of her back and drew her closer into his chest. The warmth of his body infused her through their jackets. She wanted to push closer, revel in the warmth emanating from him. His hold was light yet strong, allowing her to step back and end the embrace should she wish it.

She didn't. In fact, she wondered what was taking him so long. Her head tipped back as her body bent closer to him. The cold space between them warmed and disappeared into nothing. Of their own accord, her hands landed on his hips, sliding down to meet on his back. The muscles under her fingers clenched, and she heard Noah draw in a deep breath. His hand lingered on her face and trailed across her cheek, brushing her lower lip before curving around the side of her face. Warmth burst through her, accelerating her racing pulse.

His gaze meshed with hers, lingering on her eyes, her nose, her mouth before once more meeting her eyes. Did he like what he saw? Was he comparing her to Teneal? There was a tempest in those blue depths, the emotions swirling and combining between want, indecision, and tenderness.

"Megan," he whispered, as if knowing she needed to be assured he knew who he was with. He pressed her closer until she could feel the quick tempo of his heart beating against hers. The realization that he was as affected as she endeared him to her more. All other sounds but their rapid breathing were muted by the falling snow.

"We don't have an audience here," he whispered.

It was a question asking if this kiss was something she wanted as much as he did. It was more than that, too; it was a statement, a declaration. If she stopped him and broke their embrace, he would respect her wishes and would not push her. Would they remain friends? Did she want that?

"I don't know. Do the stars count?" she asked, smiling despite the turmoil of her thoughts.

Noah laughed gently, tipping his head back to study the expanse above them. The sky was dark, filled with thick, puffy snow clouds.

"I think we are safe with all that cloud cover," he said, stealing her breath with his intensity. He gently tipped her chin up, the loose arm around her waist tightening. Her own hands tingled as they slid up his arms and curled around his neck. Her fingers stung when they brushed against the short strands of hair at his nape. Later, she promised herself, she would ask Noah about the kiss. Right now, she wanted to experience it fully.

How would this change things between them? What did the kiss mean? She pushed all thought aside, focusing her attention on one thing only. Noah lowered his head closer to her, stopping again, his eyes silently questioning her willingness. She rose onto her toes, reducing the distance between them to no more than a breath. Breath rasped against her lips. Why had he not closed the distance?

The question must have transported to her eyes because Noah smiled. "Are you sure you want me to kiss you?"

Again, there was his consideration, her needs above his. Asking if she could accept him, all of him—past, present, and future. To her, they all made up the man; and she desperately wanted this man in her life and in this very moment to kiss her.

"Yes," she said.

Noah blinked slowly and nodded.

Then there was no more space between them as his lips pressed into hers; they were not tentative but claiming, burning hers. He groaned quietly, dropping his hand from her face, collecting her around the back of neck and pressing closer, consuming her. Megan's heart punched against her breastbone meeting Noah's beat for beat. His mouth took control, leading her deeper into the storm raging. Noah kissed like a man commanding a battle. With skill, dedication, tenacity, and passion, he kissed her, conquering her fears one by one. Even if he had not said the words, she knew by the way his mouth brushed hers that she mattered to him, that she was special to him— and that he would not compare her to Teneal, of this she was certain.

For long moments, the kiss continued in a give and take until she was a pool of emotion. Drawing once more from her mouth, he broke the kiss, chest heaving. Maybe she imagined it, but the hands molded to the small of her back trembled as they held her as if he, too, was wholly overcome from their kisses. For a long moment, he leaned his forehead against her, holding her to his chest, breathing deeply until their rasping breath slowed.

"That was . . . "

His lips found hers again. This time, the kiss was longer, deeper, and achingly sweet. When the kiss eventually slowed and they parted, Megan knew that she had been kissed in a way that she would never forget. Beside her, Noah seemed as affected by the kiss as she was.

"Noah?" she gasped, wanting to continue what they had been doing a moment before.

Noah cupped her cheek again, sliding his fingers across her cheek bones while his breath slowed. "I think we should stop there and call it a night."

A thrill whispered up Megan's spine, and she wasn't sure if it was pleasure or fear. Her smile became fuller. Noah grinned, tapped her nose gently with his finger, and pressed his forehead to hers, holding her close.

"Don't look so smug," he growled.

Megan chuckled. "If I knew my kissing skills were that good, I might have asked you to kiss me sooner."

His body froze for a few heartbeats. Then, with an almost animal rumble, she found herself being thoroughly kissed a third time.

After the longest moment, he pulled away. "I really think it's time we got you home," he said, hugging her one last time before creating much needed space between them. Her senses swam with the smell and taste of him. She nodded mutely.

"Cat got your tongue?" he teased. "Or maybe my kissing skills are far more legendary than yours."

She pushed his shoulder. "Don't get ahead of yourself," she said. "A few minutes ago, I might have thought so; but we all know my kiss makes you weak at the knees, Mr. Big Shot."

Noah's expression sobered, his eyes smoldering as he drew her into his chest again. It was a heady sensation; there was no doubt that Noah's attraction to her was almost as potent as her attraction to him. And right now, it could run away with both of them.

"That you do, Megan Davis," he said. All humor was gone from his features. "That you do."

He wisely let her go and turned her by the elbow in the direction of her car. He did not kiss her goodbye, merely watched her, his hands twitching at his side as if their need to reach out for her was as great as her need to be held by them.

"Good night, Megan," he said quietly.

"Good night, Noah."

He turned to leave and then paused, his brow bent in a frown. "I'm meeting up with Michael and the rest tomorrow to help set up for the carols evening. Would you like to come?"

Another thrill swept through her. Another date with Noah. "I'd love to."

His smile was brilliant, and she felt her own grow. Wisely, she did not move from the open door of her car but merely waved and climbed in, driving away and doing her best not to stare into her review mirror at the man standing on the sidewalk.

There was no doubt about it. After receiving the best kiss of her life, she was falling hard for Noah Thomas; and this time, she was sure she was closer to the love side of the scale than the like side she'd been on when the evening had started. As she drove, the sign above Lana's bookshop caught her gaze and led her thinking to Noah's family. What would they think of her? Would they think she was too young for their friend and brother? Or was this another one of her worries that would lead to nothing?

Chapter Twenty-Two

Noah watched as Megan's car turned the corner onto the road toward her apartment complex, the memory of their mind-blowing kisses still fresh in his mind. If there was any doubt of him going all in with Megan, it had been destroyed by kissing her tonight. Attraction was a powerful reminder of where kisses led; however, it was so much more than the chemistry between them that tipped the scale for him. It was who Megan was, what he knew of her, and the things she embodied—kindness, joy, attraction, and hope. Leaning against the hood of his truck, he looked up to the sky that was the only witness to this momentous occasion.

"So what do you think?" he said to the sky, not sure who he was addressing—God or his late wife.

Michael's words of insurmountable reasons and reforging a relationship with his Heavenly Father were never far from his mind—if he could just find out how. How did he go back after walking away from God so long ago? He already knew that God was the One Who had led him to say goodbye to Teneal, finally closing the door on that part of his past and receiving the much-needed forgiveness. That leading made a relationship with Megan possible. He was all in with Megan, but was it enough for him to be a good man and husband?

Maybe he should do what Michael suggested and pray. Maybe then he could be sure.

"Missed." Noah laughed, eating his own words as another snowball smashed into the side of his face. It was a wonder so few of Aaron and Michael's snowballs had found him today. His mind was not on the wide expanse of white, called Snowy Spring Highschool's football field, but on the young woman crouched beside him behind their makeshift snow fort.

Aaron, Michael, Sarah, and Dakota were teamed up against him and Megan in an impromptu snowball war while helping out with the preparations for the carol service at the church that evening. He'd barely slept the night before, his mind filled with little else but thoughts of the kisses he and Megan had shared and the need to get real with God. Once he had managed to tear his mind from the memory of her lips against his, he had prayed, taking all his questions and hopes to the Father above, ticking off mentally all the reasons he'd thought a relationship with Megan could not last and handing them over one by one.

It had given him some peace; however, there was still the uncertainty of the future, after all, in the beginning, his relationship with Teneal had also seemed like it would last forever. Somewhere in between, he knew he'd slept, only to awake with more questions and uncertainty. What did it take to have the peace Michael had, to trust in the plans that had been laid for him before he was born, to trust in a Father he'd known for as long as he could remember but had lost touch with over the course of years?

Megan's laughter brought him out of his reverie; and he grabbed another set of snowballs, hurling them at his brother. The action pushed aside his anxious thoughts and centered them on the woman beside him. At least, there was one thing he was sure of; Megan was here beside him for today, and that was enough. She smiled up at him, and he pushed down the urge to take her into his arms and kiss her, if only to assure himself. That would really give their audience something to talk about.

He scoffed wryly; he really did sound like a sap. He smiled back, feeling lightness enter his heart and an emotion he had not expected to ever feel again grow inside.

Another ice-packed mess crashed into Noah, spraying his already soaked head. He gasped, glaring playfully at his brother.

Michael's eyes widened before he laughed so hard, he nearly fell over.

"Eyes up, Noah." He gasped.

"You're asking for it, bro." Noah bent down, gathering a mess of snow and slush ready to lob it straight at his brother's amused face.

Ever grateful for his future sister-in-law, Noah saw Sarah wink at him, grab a handful of slushy mess from under her feet, and plaster it all over her fiancé's face. Michael's laughter cut off abruptly. He turned to Sarah creeping closer, his arms stretched out wide. Sarah squealed.

"Michael Thomas, don't you—" Her words were cut off as Michael lunged, crashing himself and Sarah into a nearby snow dune and cutting off her words with his mouth. They kissed for a long moment until Aaron grabbed another snowball and threw it at them, covering them in a thin layer of white powder.

"Come on, you guys! The wedding isn't until next month; spare the rest of us, please."

The kiss came to an end with a loud swack; and Michael pushed up to standing, pulling Sarah up with him. Her cheeks blazed red. They dusted the excess snow from their jackets and jeans, and then Michael drew Sarah into his arms.

"Do you guys need some time alone?" Noah asked.

Michael roughly cleared his throat, facing a blushing Sarah. "No, we're good."

It didn't take a genius to figure out what was going on. The act of marriage was sacred to both Michael and Sarah; his brother had spoken of it to him. With the time before the wedding growing less and less, they were struggling to keep their heads when alone together. An unsettling feeling built in his chest. He and Teneal had not honored any of those covenants before their wedding day. Could that have been a reason their marriage was doomed to fail? He reached for Megan, needing her close. Clasping her gloved hand in his and drawing her into his side, he silently made a promise to himself and Megan. If their relationship should progress to the point of marriage, he would do everything in his power to honor her in that way. He'd promised her as much when they had started dating.

"Are you guys coming tonight?" Michael asked, once the awkward moment had passed.

Noah turned to Megan. "Do you want to come with me tonight?"

Unable to withstand the temptation with her so close, he gently kissed her cheek, appreciating the color that filled her cheeks at his actions. He didn't suppress his smile.

"Yes, I'd love to come," she said, watching him with eyes filled with longing. Megan had made it very clear how much she did not like audiences when they kissed; however, he was having trouble remembering that there were people witnessing their exchange when her eyes were holding his in this way. The desire to ignore the world and do exactly what she was silently asking almost overwhelmed him.

"Maybe later," he whispered, drawing a blush from her.

"You sound awfully sure of yourself," she murmured.

"What can I say? I can't get enough of your legendary kissing skills." He kissed her forehead quickly.

Megan snorted; and he laughed out loud, turning back to Michael. "What time does the service start?"

"Seven o' clock," he said.

"We'll be there," he said. "I don't know about you guys, but I think my old bones have had enough cold for one afternoon. I think I need something hot to warm me up."

"Sounds good. Sarah and I have an appointment with a wedding cake baker." Michael kissed Sarah on the cheek as they waved their goodbyes. That left the party down to four.

"You ready to call it?" Aaron asked, looking down at his diminutive girlfriend, Dakota.

"I think I've had enough snow and ice for one day." She shivered, smiling brightly at Aaron, who got a dopey look on his face. He wrapped his arms around her and held her to his chest.

"I guess that's us, too," Aaron said.

"You ready to go?" Noah asked Megan.

"Am I ever! I think my hands are going to fall off!"

Noah looked at Megan's hands, taking them into his. He removed his gloves and hers and then gently rubbed warmth into their joined hands.

"Better?"

Megan smiled and nodded.

"So, we'll see you later at the church?" Aaron asked, his arm around Dakota's back.

"Yeah, we will be there."

Noah nodded his greeting to Aaron and Dakota, leading Megan away from the football field and into the large high school that had been his home for four years. As much as he would have liked to keep Megan out on that cold field and indulge in some of that kissing on both their minds, indoors seemed a far more pleasant way to spend more time with her. He was wet from the snowball fight; and if he wasn't careful, he would have a one-way ticket to hypothermia in the current temperatures. The stump attached to his prosthetic leg was already aching from the strenuous activity of earlier that, combined with the cold, made it sure he was in for a painful night unless he did as Brett suggested and took some time to rest and warm the leg. Oh well, he would worry about that later.

They walked through the empty hallways hand in hand past the classrooms where he'd been taught calculus, kinesiology, and band.

He stopped outside one of the classrooms, pushing open the door.

"This was my history class," he said.

The room smelled exactly as he remembered it, like marker fumes, B.O., and dust. In his mind's eye, he saw high school him sitting beside high school Teneal, at once realizing that the pain that had always accompanied such memories was less. It wasn't gone—and he knew it would never be gone—but it didn't hold the painful sting it had in the weeks before. It didn't have the clawing effect it had always had on him. For the first time, he knew he had finally put his past with Teneal to rest. He was ready to see where things would go with Megan.

With that thought burning in him, he guided Megan from the room, closed the door, and drew her into his arms, forgetting about his earlier hesitancy to kiss her. He lovingly pressed his lips to hers, tenderly, slowly drawing out the emotions she arose in him. *Forever,* his heart said, and he couldn't help agreeing. He was in love with Megan. Maybe he had been from the moment he'd met her, and it had taken him this long for his head to catch up; or maybe it was the night he had gone to say his final goodbye to Teneal that his heart had been ready to accept another. Whenever it had happened, he would do everything in his power to protect it and love Megan with everything he had. He hoped that it would be enough.

When the kiss slowed and he pulled away, Megan looked at him questioningly. He shook his head silently—not because he didn't want her to know of his revelation but because he wanted the time to do things right with Megan. He would take the time to woo her and hopefully make her fall in love with him, too. He didn't think that task would be impossible. Megan was not a woman who went around kissing anyone; and that meant that if she was kissing him with the passion she was, there was a level of emotion involved. But was it love?

"Are you ready to go?" he asked.

Megan nodded. "Noah, are you okay?"

He should have known she would sense the change in the feel of his kisses. Cupping her cheeks in his hands, he kissed her again. "Yes." If only she knew how okay he really was. But soon. Soon, he would tell her and find out if the depth of his feelings were the same as hers.

In silence, they walked to his truck. He started up the engine, turning up the heat to maximum; the weather station had promised clear skies and sub-zero temperatures for the next few days. Noah grimaced at the thought of working out in those conditions. Christmas was less than two weeks away, and business was booming at the farm. Buck had agreed to allow Michael and Aaron, when they had the time to, help Noah with the sanitizing and baling of trees so that all orders could be met on time. He looked over at Megan, her expression still bent in question.

"Is something wrong?" she asked as he pulled off from the school and joined the main road. Noah reached over the seat; taking her hand into his again, he lifted her hand to his mouth and kissed her knuckles.

"No, I think everything is finally going to be all right."

When he dropped her off at her apartment, he kissed her again gently, not wanting to ignite the fire that would undoubtedly steal his sense and set her away from him.

"Would 6:30 p.m. be okay to come get you?"

Megan nodded. She hugged him one last time. He wrapped his arms around her, burrowing his face into her neck, taking in her sweet scent, and marveling at how she felt now that he'd allowed himself to give into the joy of holding her.

"I'll see you later," he said quietly and then let go of her and turned to his truck. He pushed the gear into drive before his control left and he confessed everything to her.

Chapter Twenty-Three

She was in love with Noah Thomas, and it terrified her. Megan sank into her love seat and aimlessly flicked on the TV, hoping to distract her from her lingering questions. Something had happened to Noah as they wandered around the school, something that when he'd looked at her, her heart had stalled in her chest and then was off to the races. The tender light in his eyes and the almost reverent way his hands cupped her back when he kissed her made her suspect that perhaps their journey into his past would bring memories of his time with Teneal to the forefront of his memory. However, whatever memory he'd discovered had nothing to do with Teneal and everything, it seemed, to do with Megan. Her stomach quivered at the thought of how he made her feel. When had her like level changed to love? And was Noah truly over his wife and ready to move on with her?

The ringing doorbell unexpectedly intruded on her busy thoughts. Megan sighed, placed the cup of hazelnut cream coffee on the table, and rose to answer it.

"Tyreke?" she said, opening the door wider to allow her brother entrance into the apartment. "Aren't you supposed to be at the hospital?"

He didn't answer, just brushed past her and sank tiredly into the loveseat she had just vacated. He sighed deeply, resting his head between his hands. His clothes were rumpled, and there was a small milk stain on the side of his shirt pocket. His whole demeanor spoke of hopelessness and crushing grief. What was wrong?

"What is it, Tyreke? What's wrong?"

She sat down beside him and laid a hand on the tense muscles of his arms. After drawing a few deep breaths, he blew them out heavily as if trying to calm something inside him. When his gaze rose to meet hers, it was teary and lined with exhaustion. This was really bad.

"I just came from there," he said quietly, in answer to her question. His gaze held hers, silently communicating, and she knew. She just knew whatever news he'd come to deliver was far from good. She linked her hand with his.

"Just tell me," she said. "Did something happen to Mr. Ambrose?"

Tyreke's hand convulsed in hers, and his breath began to rasp again through his chest. "It's bad, Megs, really bad." There was terrible agony in his brown eyes, so much like her own.

A shiver raced up her spine, and she swallowed back her own rising emotions. "How bad?"

"One week," he croaked, his pain leaking into his voice. "The doctors have given him one week. The treatment has done nothing to stop the spread of the cancer. They hoped it at least would give him a bit more time, but . . . " His voice broke with a crackle.

Tyreke swallowed hard and drew another long breath, releasing it heavily from his chest. "Mia can't stop crying. I don't know how to tell Isaiah that his grandpa is going to die."

He rolled his shoulders, trying to release the stress there; it was unbearable to witness. "Amana just sits there quietly praying. We all put on a good face when we're at the hospital, but at home . . . " His voice trailed off again, and Megan guessed what happened when there was no need for pretense. Wasn't she an expert at it?

She released her brother's hand and drew him into her arms in a hug. He exhaled, accepting the embrace, and then wrapped his own arms around her so they sat side by side.

"I hoped Isaiah would be able to get to know his grandpa growing up." Another wave of emotion slammed into her brother, and he barely caught it in time to stop another ragged sob rising from him.

Megan felt her own pain pierce her. Although she'd been expecting the news, it was still hard to hear. From the beginning, they'd known that Mr. Ambrose's cancer would ultimately end his life and that any kind of treatment would be too late, but she'd hoped . . . They all had. Emotions squeezed her own throat; and she swallowed it back, crushing her own tears. She could not give into tears now, not when her brother needed her.

Silence filled the room, and they sat. Megan thought about praying; she'd thought about it a great deal since her discussion with Mr. Ambrose, remembering the comfort she had found when surrounded by the low voices of Mia and Mrs. Ambrose at the hospital.

God, if You're out there . . . She didn't know what else to say but hoped if God truly knew everything, He would know what she couldn't express.

Tyreke's ragged breathing gradually slowed as the metal gray of the afternoon faded into a dull pastel purple of the evening outside her window. Megan's mind returned repeatedly to that conversation in the hospital.

"He's at peace with dying, Ty. I think the best thing we can do is to make peace with that, too."

Her brother stiffened beside her; but before he could speak, she continued, "I know it sounds crazy; but maybe, he's onto something. I mean, I don't necessarily agree with his ideas or his Jesus or Heaven; but after all the research I've done, I think Mr. Ambrose is onto something." She ran her hand through her messy hair, trying to put into words her own scattered thoughts. "If he wasn't, why would he be so happy?"

Tyreke remained quiet for a long time, his pensive gaze holding hers, confusion clear in the bend of his brow.

"Since when did you lose your skepticism?" he asked, cocking his head to the side. "When Mom and Dad died, you were adamant that they were stolen from us; and as far as I know, you've been holding onto that vendetta against God since then. What changed?"

When he said it like that, it did sound crazy coming from her. She didn't know exactly when her point of view had begun to change. Was it when she'd heard Noah's story and struggles for the first time? Was it when she'd finally realized her own struggles? Was it when she'd eventually been brave enough to share those struggles with Mr. Ambrose? Or was it merely that she needed something to hold onto when facing death again? Mr. Ambrose was so sure of his course, so sure of what awaited him, a guarantee of something after this life.

When her words did not make it her lips, Tyreke pressed on. "Why is it so important to you that there is something after death?" If possible, his expression grew more haggard; and Megan recognized the same desperation she felt reflected in his dark eyes, so much like her own.

"Because . . . " The only real reason she could come up with was, "Because it gives me hope."

"Well, that's . . . " Tyreke's mouth closed and then opened again, only to close again. He drew a deep breath. "I guess that's better than nothing. Mia always talks about God and that kind of stuff but . . . " He shrugged, tousling his own messy hair.

"But you haven't found a reason or situation where it makes sense to you? Makes you believe?" she finished for him.

Tyreke nodded. "Yeah." He squeezed Megan's hand, rising to his feet. "George's cancer has really got me thinking." He paused and then grinned down at her. "I guess it has you thinking, too, huh?"

"Nah," she said rising beside him. "I've been thinking about this for a long time—sometimes to the point of obsession," she admitted a little sheepishly. She shrugged. "It might give us both some closure if we stopped thinking so much and just believed."

"That's what Amana says." He chuckled fondly at the thought his mother-in-law, and Megan was relieved to see that some of the weight he'd walked in with a few hours ago was lifting from him. The dark cloud was giving way to some sunshine.

"I always said you'd married well."

Tyreke's chuckle turned into a laugh. "You know, I did." He rose. "I guess it's time for me to get back. Thanks, Megs, I didn't really say how much we appreciate your help with everything that's been going on."

"I am just glad I could help. I know how much stress you and Mia have been under; it was the least I could do. Do you need me to get Isaiah tonight?"

"No, Amana is staying at the hospital tonight, and Mia and I will be home."

As they crossed the room en route back to her door, Megan turned to see her brother watching her again. He rubbed his chin but still didn't speak; he just stared like he was assessing her. He wanted to know something and wasn't sure how to ask for the information.

"Okay, what is it?" she asked.

"Nothing, just . . . " He went silent again.

"Ty, I know that look. What is it?"

"Mia tells me she thinks you are seeing someone. Naturally, I thought she was crazy. I mean, you are way too busy for relationships. Right?" He raised his eyebrow in question.

"Let me guess. You phoned Grace again, didn't you?"

He leaned back against the door frame. "What? I worry about you. It's a brother's right to worry about his little sister, isn't it?" He innocently smiled, but she could see his mind working.

"Relax, big bro," she said wryly, raising her pointer and middle fingers like bunny ears for emphasis. "It's new, and there is nothing you need to worry about."

Her brother's arms lifted to cross over his chest, his expression growing serious. "Name?"

"Ty."

"Name, Megan."

"That's none of your business. Now, if you please," she tried with some success to pull her door open and unceremoniously shove her brother out into the hallway. The door opened a crack—not enough to have a hope of getting Tyreke through it. Megan tried again. Tyreke wasn't having it; he might as well have been a large boulder, for all the effect she had on him. "Name, Megan, or I'll be here all night."

"You can't. Mia's waiting for you to get home."

"Name, Megan," he insisted.

"Okay, I'll tell you his name if you get out of my apartment. I have somewhere I need to be in an hour."

This made Tyreke's expression harden further; however, he walked out and stood in her doorway, waiting for her answer. She knew her brother, and he wasn't going to budge unless she told him. Giving into the inevitable, she sighed.

"Noah Thomas."

His eyebrows rose to his hairline, but one nod was all the response her brother gave. "Be careful, Megs," he said.

"I will. Love you, Ty."

"Love you, too." With that, he turned on his heel and headed for the exit.

While Megan got ready for her date with Noah, her thoughts stayed on her family and the loss they would face in fewer days than any one of them were prepared for. And her discussion with Tyreke— what if she did stop questioning and just believe? It sounded too simple to her sometimes overly analytical mind. Mr. Ambrose was a smart man, and no one would easily pull the wool over his eyes in anything; and yet he believed.

She could see it in his face when he'd spoken of his Jesus and Heaven. Not for a moment did he doubt what he believed. The same could be said for Mia and Mrs. Ambrose; they, too, believed fully in their God. Tyreke and Megan had always been the skeptics; their parents had been no different. She had wondered what it was like to grow up in a household that believed in Someone higher than themselves, that had such surety in their faith. Maybe then, the thought of trusting in that Higher Power would not be so foreign to her. Sighing, she pushed the thoughts to the back of her mind; she would have time to consider them later.

Megan exchanged her jeans for dressy black pants and her sweater for a deep red blouse, slipping her feet into her black boots. She fluffed her hair a few times while applying a light layer of makeup. Nerves danced in her stomach, and she breathed deeply. Of all the times she and Noah had been out, she'd known what to expect. However, the service at the church was a first for her, and she wasn't sure how to act or what would be expected of her.

The doorbell rang. It was time for her date.

Chapter Twenty-Four

Twinkling white lights lit up every corner of the packed church as old and well-sung Christmas hymns serenaded from the modern sound system. Noah shifted his shoulders, trying to release some of the tension in them. Although he'd made in roads to renewing his relationship with his Savior, he still felt like a wandering sheep in need of the firm hand of the Shepherd. He drew Megan closer to his side and felt something deep and warm fill his chest when she snuggled closer. Her eyes were tired and looked as if she'd been crying recently.

"Are you sure you're okay? We can go back to your apartment if you don't feel up to tonight," he asked for the fifth time since he'd met her at her apartment, his arriving coinciding with Tyreke's leaving.

The short and long of it was that things at the hospital were not going well; and soon, Megan would once again have to say goodbye to someone she loved. The thought cut through him, and he felt a new sense of responsibility alongside the overpowering love he had for Megan. He would be there for her whatever was to come. She would not be alone. And judging by the weighing look he had received after being introduced to her brother, Tyreke, he'd be watched every step of the way. He didn't mind. He knew all about brothers; he could handle Tyreke.

"Yes, I'm fine. Better than fine." She quickly lifted to her tippy toes and kissed him on his cheek. "Thanks for worrying," she said softly.

There was a heaviness to her words, like something was on her mind. Should he ask her about it? No, he would give her the privacy she needed. If she needed to talk, he was sure she would let him know.

He brushed his lips across her forehead, pleased as she leaned into the touch while suppressing the urge to turn the quick kiss into one that was much for fulfilling. He could only imagine the interest that would bring. No doubt, the people arriving for the Carols by Candlelight service would not appreciate their PDA moment.

Gently placing pressure on Megan's lower back, he guided her over to a set of pews in the middle of the church. The row was already half-full with Aaron, Dakota, Lana, Sarah, and Michael. He did a doubletake at the sight of his brothers Levi and Drew entering the church and nonchalantly filling up the rest of the row. Noah raised his eyebrow in question. In response, Levi and Drew smiled, their gazes full of significance as they took in Noah and Megan holding hands. What were they doing here?

He groaned softly as he caught the huge smile on Michael's face. Michael raised his eyebrows innocently and shrugged as if it was no big deal. *Great. Just great.* His first relationship in a while and already his family were sticking their noses in where they didn't belong. He wasn't angry; it was inevitable with a family as close and as big as the Thomases.

"Looks like we are in for the Spanish Inquisition later," he said, leaning close to her ear, his voice low. He traveled his gaze to his brothers, nodding.

Megan's body stiffened, her eyes wide and questioning. "Who are they?" she asked, letting go of his hand and putting some space between their bodies. Noah wasn't having any of it. He curled his arm around her shoulders and brought her back into his chest.

"The rest of the Thomas brothers," Noah said, pressing his nose into her hair. "Have I told you how much I like the shampoo you use? What is it?"

"Not so quickly, buddy." She grinned. "I know when someone is trying to distract me." She poked him in the ribs, and he groaned quietly again.

"What was that for?" he asked in mock pain.

She shifted against him again, her agitation clear in the way she wove her fingers in and out of his. All humor drained from her expression; and her face became pensive, worry clear in those deep brown eyes.

"Megan? Are you okay?"

"What do they know about me?" she asked, her voice laced with uncertainty. Leaning closer, Noah gently kissed her cheek.

"Nothing further than what I suppose Michael and Sarah have told them. I am as surprised as you to see them here tonight. I think the news of their grumpy older brother having a girlfriend is the reason they came. One thing you should know about my family is they are extremely nosy and love to meddle in each other's lives. We all do it or have done it. I even did my part to try and get Michael and Sarah to see their feelings for each other."

His words didn't seem to appease Megan at all; in fact, the worry in her eyes intensified. Tenderness arose in him at her distress; and he cupped her shoulder, slowly lacing his fingers with hers. "Please don't worry; they mean well. I promise it will be fine."

Megan swallowed hard, glanced once more at the row of people beside them, and then nodded and put on a brave face.

Love for her swelled in his chest, and he hoped it would reflect into his words. "Megan, they'll love you." *Just like I do,* he added silently. A sweet kiss on her forehead and he sat back in his seat, turning to the front of the room, their hands still entwined.

After a long moment, Megan sighed, relaxing into him and doing the same. The noise level settled into a soft hum as the lights around the room went out one by one, leaving only the soft glow of white Christmas lights illuminating the space. The gentle strands of "O Holy Night" swelled from the band. Noah felt himself being transported back in time to a place when his life was simple and his faith innocent and childlike. Forgetting all about his brothers and the upcoming meeting between them and Megan, he let the music take him as he rose to sing with the rest of the congregation.

A heavy pressure built behind his eyes, increasing as he allowed the words to flow over him, the telltale signs of tears wetting his cheeks.

His knees buckled as his hands slapped into the wooden back of the pew, bracing himself. The weight of his choices pressing, pressing, pressing.

The weight was terrible, blending with his pain. His slavery was not of man but of himself, of the past of his mistakes. His tears merged into rivulets carving a chasm into his chest where a heart of stone resided. They washed over the darkness that had taken root, there cleansing it.

There was nothing more of himself to hold back, nothing more that was hidden if only from himself. God knew it all and loved him, anyway. He swallowed again, harder, fighting through the deluge of emotions, lifting a hand to wipe the evidence of his reckoning from his face. It was done; he was clean.

I love you; you are Mine. A quiet Voice whispered in his heart; and for the first time in years, Noah knew the truth of all he'd learned in Sunday school and his parents' house as a child. God loved him and had called him back. The chasm of years Noah had put between them was not wide enough that the love of Christ could not cross it and find him.

I'm sorry, Lord. Please forgive me. I recommit my life to You. Noah drew a deep breath, suppressing the urge to laugh at the lightness that now invaded his chest. He could finally let go of the past—of Teneal and all the mistakes he'd made in those years—and he could begin again. His eyes drifted to the woman beside him, his relieved smile growing wide at the concern he saw in her eyes.

"Are you okay?" she asked softly, leaning close as the music continued in the background.

"Yes," he said, allowing the lightness in his chest to carry over to his face. Megan's worried expression became stunned for a moment before it transformed into a full, beautiful smile. He found himself equally stunned, the words he'd come to terms with that afternoon on the tip of his tongue. As the song ended, Noah placed a kiss on her forehead again and turned back. Now was not the time to share what was on his heart; but soon, it would be. He knew it.

Another carol started up, swallowing any chance he had of putting his thoughts into action. A more private setting might be better to reveal the words on his heart, even though he wanted to shout them from the rooftop. But now, he would rest in the fact that he was loved and finally had come home after being gone for so many years.

The open notes of "Angels We Have Heard on High" swelled through the room, and he lifted his voice along with the ones melodic around him with a new lightness of praise and thanks singing the familiar words. The last line rang as the song ended; and he glanced down at Megan, frowning at her pensive expression. Her beautiful eyes were wet, her gaze far away. Emotions flickered like a movie reel over her expressive features. The Holy Spirit was working on his love. A joy like none other burst into his chest, thankfulness fresh and new. Leaving the Spirit to its work, he curled Megan tighter into his side and continued to sing. Maybe tonight, they both would find their way home.

Happy and emotionally spent, Noah walked with Megan toward his truck after the service.

"Hey, Noah, aren't you going to introduce us?" Levi called, dragging a grinning Drew with him.

"Here we go," he muttered. "Lord, give me strength."

Megan giggled beside him. She'd been practically glued to his side for most of the evening; and every time she was away from him, he just wanted to be beside her again. Man, he had it bad, and he loved it.

"Megan, these two knuckleheads are my brothers Drew and Levi. They live in Denver, where my parents are."

"It's so nice to meet you both," Megan said, reaching out to shake each of his brothers' hands. "What brings you to Snowy Springs?"

Drew glanced at Levi, grinning. Noah shook his head; here came something embarrassing.

"Well, when Michael called and told us that Noah was worked up about a woman, we didn't believe him. Our grumpy Noah, tied up over a woman, was not possible," Drew said. "Michael insisted, and we came to see it for ourselves."

"All right, that's enough. Don't you two have somewhere else to be—like, I don't know, back in Denver?" Noah asked, heat filling his cheeks.

"Is that so?" Megan glanced up, dazzling him with the look in her eyes. Did he dare hope that she felt the way about him as he did about her?

Levi shared a few stories from their childhood, embarrassing Noah until he thought he might thump his brother just to get him to stop. However, Megan seemed to be enjoying their company, and he didn't have the heart to pull her away. An hour later, Megan yawned; and he knew this was his cue to take her home. They bid goodnight to everyone and climbed into his truck.

"Should I apologize for them?" he asked when they were on the road to Megan's apartment, their joined hands resting on his thigh.

She giggled. "No, it was nice to meet them. You guys remind me a lot of Tyreke and me; we would do anything for each other. And as I am sure you saw earlier, we are just as present in each other's lives as your family is."

"They can be a bit overwhelming sometimes, but we all have a great relationship with each other and our parents."

Megan shook her head. "Even then, you are lucky to have them and parents who love you."

Noah paused and drew a deep breath. "Megan, I'm sorry. I didn't—"

She waved his concern away. "It's okay, Noah. My parents are gone, and there is nothing I can do to bring them back. I don't say that to make you feel sorry for me; there are days that are hard and days that are easier. Recently, though, the days have been harder."

"I'm sorry, Megan. I wish there was some way I could make it better."

Deep color filled Megan's cheeks. She glanced down at her hands, up at him, and then at her hands again. Noah's heart thrummed in his chest.

"Megan?"

"Being with you has made it better. You have no idea how much."

Thankful that they had reached Megan's apartment building, Noah pulled the truck to park, switched off the engine, and pulled Megan into his arms, kissing her with all the emotion in his heart.

Chapter Twenty-Five

"How can I help?" Megan asked Mrs. Ambrose as the older woman hustled around the room. Her dark skin shone lightly with perspiration, her cheeks rosy.

She smiled warmly. "No, thank you, Megan. You just go out there and make sure that old coot doesn't injure himself."

Megan grinned, pushing open the kitchen door entering the living room.

"I heard that," Mr. Ambrose said from somewhere in the room.

Mrs. Ambrose chuckled softly, her face tender and vulnerable. She suddenly swallowed hard and nodded at Megan, her dark eyes speaking volumes. Megan understood. They all did. It was Christmas day, and they were running out of time. Two days ago, the doctors had sent Mr. Ambrose home with enough pain medication to sink a ship and a personal support worker who came in the mornings and evenings to check on him. There was no sign of recovery, but there was nothing more the doctors could do.

The older man, stubborn as he was, was adamant that he would not spend his last days in a hospital where strange people came and went at all hours of the day and night. If he was going to be sent home to his Savior, he would do it in his own bed, in his own house. The trip back home had been bittersweet knowing this.

Sighing, Megan crossed the room to where Mr. Ambrose sat, Mia beside him, Isaiah asleep on his lap. Her heart clenched in her chest as she watched him and Mia interact quietly. He was careful to not stir the infant on his lap. From behind her, a warm hand encircled her waist; and Megan couldn't hold back the smile the feeling brought. Noah stared down at her, his eyes filled with the same sorrow she was sure was reflected in her own eyes.

His mouth lifted into a tender smile. "Are you okay?" he mouthed.

She nodded and swallowed back her tears, determined to make whatever days Mr. Ambrose had left filled with joy and laughter. Winding her hand into the fingers at her waist, she led Noah closer. At their approach, Mr. Ambrose stopped his discussion with Mia turning his attention to them.

"And who might this be?" Mr. Ambrose asked, handing the sleeping child over to Tyreke, who cuddled Isaiah to his chest and crossed the room to where the Christmas tree stood. It was only half-decorated, and Tyreke was doing his best to remedy that problem before Christmas dinner happened.

"Noah Thomas, sir," Noah said, stepping forward and warmly clasping the older man's hand. Mr. Ambrose shook it; and then once Noah had taken a stepped back, he lifted an enquiring eyebrow at Megan. She felt her cheeks fill with color.

"Noah and I are seeing each other," she said shyly, unsure of why she felt like a young girl introducing her dad to her high school boyfriend. Maybe it was because finally the relationship between her and Mr. Ambrose had changed to one that resembled a parent and child. Since the night where she'd laid her heart bare, something had shifted between them, something that filled her heart with gratitude but also with a deep grief knowing that soon Mr. Ambrose would leave this earth.

With some effort, she pushed the thought aside. *Enjoy the time you have left; stop dwelling on the future.* The action was easier said than done. Or maybe it was just the nerves that came with first-time introductions.

"Oh," Mr. Ambrose said, giving Noah the once-over. "Hey, Amana, did you know our other daughter brought home a fella?"

"Yes, George," Mrs. Ambrose said from the kitchen.

"Why didn't you tell me she had a fella?"

"Because I only met him just before you did." Mrs. Ambrose stopped in the doorway between the two rooms. "Now, don't you give the poor boy a hard time. Show Megan you've got manners," she said, smiling before turning back into the kitchen.

"I would never," Mr. Ambrose said, smiling widely. "Well, come over here, Noah Thomas, and tell me how you met our Megan."

Leaving the two men to their discussion, Megan turned toward where Tyreke and Isaiah stood. Tyreke glanced over his shoulder at her before turning and handing her a long string of bright red tinsel.

"He seems nice," Tyreke said. "Older?"

Megan groaned quietly. "You, too?"

Tyreke widened his eyes in innocence. "What? He is older than you."

"Yes, and . . ."

"I don't know. It seems an odd match, the two of you. Are you sure you want to be involved with someone like that?"

Megan swung her gaze, watching Noah as he gestured at something he was trying to explain to Mr. Ambrose. She still hadn't told Noah she loved him, but she could feel it leaking out of her in waves.

"I love him," she said quietly, almost afraid that if she admitted it out loud, something would happen to the beauty of the emotions she felt. In that moment, Noah glanced up at her, smiling softly with that light in his eyes from the other day. She didn't know what it was exactly, but she hoped it was what she thought it was—that Noah loved her like she loved him. She wasn't sure how he felt, but . . .

Tyreke coughed and then reached to pat Isaiah on the back gently calming the squirming infant. "When did this happen? And why am I only finding out about it right this moment?"

Megan shrugged. "I don't know," she admitted. "Sometime in the last week or so—maybe in the last month? I wasn't looking for it, you know?" She trailed her gaze back to her brother, picking up another pair of decorations and hanging them on the tree.

"Love rarely happens when we're looking for it," Tyreke said, his eyes fixed on Mia. She'd left Noah and her father to their discussion and was now moving busily around the dinner table laying out the tablecloth and settings. As if sensing his gaze, she smiled softly at Tyreke. For the first time, Megan understood what her brother and his wife had and maybe, in some part, all of what they had faced in their years together.

"Does he feel the same?"

"I think so," she said.

"But you're not sure?"

"Well, I can't exactly go up to him and say, 'Hey, I love you; do you feel the same?' It's not like we're in elementary school with a paper that says if you like me, check the box."

Tyreke chuckled. The sound strangled off with a low whistle. He was looking at something over her shoulder. She froze, becoming very aware of the warm presence at her back. Turning slowly, she lifted her head to meet Noah's gaze. It was liquid blue swimming again with that emotion she hoped for but couldn't name.

"Noah?" she asked softly.

Noah didn't answer her, merely wrapped his large hand around her waist, turning her into his chest. He sighed softly and then said, "Tyreke, do you mind if I borrow Megan for a while?"

"By all means."

He turned them toward the front door of the Ambrose home, leading her forward.

"Don't forget your coats," Tyreke called after them.

Noah doubled back toward the hall closet, collecting his and Megan's coats as they reached the door. Silently, he helped her into her coat, zipping up the front, not looking at her, not saying a word.

Her heart sank. He'd heard what she said, and he was going to let her down softly. That's why they were going outside. He didn't want an audience for what she'd inadvertently forced him to do. He didn't love her. He cared about her—of that much she was sure—but care and love did not equate to the same thing. Noah zipped up his coat and then opened the front door, ushering her through it onto the snow-covered lawn out front.

It was snowing again; flourishes of white patterns filled the air, deadening all sound around them. The Christmas lights from the houses in the neighborhood glowed softly in falling powder.

"Look, Noah," she said, stopping him at the steps of the porch.

Noah gently placed a finger over her lips. He gazed at her a long time, eyes soft, gentle, and burning into hers. At last, he drew a deep breath, drawing her slowly into his arms and placing a soft kiss on her forehead, then on her cheek bones—first the right, then the left—then another kiss on her nose, and finally slipping his mouth along her jaw until his mouth was an inch away from hers. She felt the warmth of his breath brush over her mouth.

"I love you," he whispered. He chuckled, softly brushing his mouth lightly against hers. "I was hoping to say it differently and had this grand idea formed about how it would happen. But it seems you beat me to it."

"Noah . . . I . . . uh . . . " She drew in a deep breath. "Are you sure . . . I mean . . . .it's only been . . . " His kiss cut off anything else she might have said. She melted into the sensation, pressing closer to deepen the kiss. Oh boy, did the man know how to kiss.

"I love you," he said between kisses. She kissed him once more and then, with restraint, drew away. "Wait, I need to tell you to your face."

Noah paused. "What?"

"You mean, you didn't hear?"

Noah remained silent, smiling. He had heard; he just wanted her to say it. Drawing another deep breath, Megan lifted to her tippy toes so her eyes lined up with his.

"I love you, Noah Thomas."

"And I love you, Megan Davis."

Eye's glowing with tenderness, Noah dipped his hand into his pocket and drew out a small ribbon-covered box. "I was going to give this to you later, but now seems like a much better time."

Megan lifted the box from his outstretched hand and lifted the lid. A glittering silver bracelet lay surrounded by a soft cotton-like cushion, and at the center was a red stone. The word *hope* was engraved on the surface.

"Noah, this is beautiful. Thank you."

"I don't know if it makes me sound like the sap that Michael claims I am. But when I saw that bracelet, I was looking for hope; and I know you were, too. I think that God kept on placing us together knowing that we would help each other find it."

Megan nodded and melted into his kiss, knowing in her heart that what he said was true.

Chapter Twenty-Six

"I'm at the hospital. Can you come?" Megan's voice sounded frantic over the phone line, squeezing Noah's heart at the pain in her voice.

"Just let me tell Buck, and then I'll be on my way."

Megan ended the call with a short "love you," and Noah hurt for her. The last week with her had been one of the happiest he'd had in a long time. They'd spent every moment together when Megan wasn't either at school, the hospital, or work. On New Year's Eve, Mr. Ambrose had taken a turn for the worst and was readmitted to Snowy Medical Hospital. They all knew that this would be the last; he would not be coming home again.

Jogging carefully, as much as his leg would allow, he raced toward the farmhouse, slapping his boots against the welcome mat to shift the layers of snow.

"Buck, you here?" he asked.

"In the study."

Noah quickly shucked his jacket and boots and walked quickly to the room where Buck sat behind a large oak desk, his head bent over a pile of papers. Small circular spectacles perched on his nose.

"I need to leave for the day," Noah said.

Buck nodded. "The reason?"

"Megan called. Mr. Ambrose is not doing well."

Buck nodded slowly. "Go. I'll call Michael and see if he can lend a hand today."

"Already did. He's on his way."

"Thank you, Noah. Drive safely."

"Will do."

Minutes later, Noah was on his way to the hospital, praying that whatever was to happen that Megan's family would know peace in their grief.

The reception desk was empty, the hallway eerily quiet. He hurried down the corridor to the room Megan had messaged him, hoping that he was in time to be beside Megan when the dear old man he'd met only a week ago went home to his Lord.

The soft sound of weeping greeted his ears as he opened the door. Megan rushed into his arms as he came into the fully occupied room. He hugged her close, breathing in her soft scent, his heart beating painfully in his chest for the tears that wet his shirt. In a circle around the bed, Mia stood beside her mother, Isaiah in her arms, Tyreke on her other side, holding his wife close to his side. Looping his arm around Megan's back, Noah moved closer to the bed. Mr. Ambrose lay chest unmoving, a peaceful expression on his aged face.

"He went a few minutes ago," Megan said quietly. Noah nodded, a lump of grief forming in his throat.

"I'm sorry," he said, drawing her into another hug, placing a soft kiss on her forehead. "I know how much you loved him."

Megan pressed her face more firmly into his shoulder, swallowing hard, her body stiff. He soothed his hand up and down her back until she drew a deep breath and stepped away. Her expression was closed; her eyes that usually sparkled were pained. He stared down at her, holding her gaze until she nodded, stepping back. He pressed his lips to her forehead again, releasing her to walk over to where Mia, Tyreke, and Mrs. Ambrose stood.

"I am so sorry for your loss," he said quietly to them.

"He is at peace," Mrs. Ambrose said, her voice filled with unushered tears. Mia wept quietly beside her, tucked close into Tyreke's side.

"Thank you," Tyreke said, reaching over to shake Noah's hand.

"Is there anything I can do?" he asked.

Tyreke shook his head "We're waiting for the people from the funeral home to arrive to take George away," he said.

Tyreke's voice was strong and steady, but Noah could hear the wealth of suppressed emotion behind it. This family was hurting, and he knew there were no words he could say that would help soothe their pain. Grief was a process, one which took time and patience to work through. Standing beside Megan, he could sense her need to just be in this moment. She was fighting some internal battle, and he wished he knew how he could help.

Two tense hours of silence later, broken only by one or two rapid whispers, the men from the funeral home arrived and took Mr. Ambrose away. Noah understood the stark pain he saw on Amana Ambrose's face as they wheeled her husband away. He hadn't even seen Teneal before the day of the funeral. Noah drew a deep breath and blew it out.

"Can I take you home?" he asked Megan, taking one of her hands into his and turning her to face him. Her hands were ice. She'd been standing for the past thirty minutes staring out the hospital window, glancing periodically over her shoulder at Mr. Ambrose's still form.

She nodded, collecting her things. She said a quiet goodbye, hugging each of her family members close as they parted in the opposite direction, and then followed him out the door. They silently walked from the hospital out to his truck. The cutting wind had not let up, and the sky remained a dove gray mixed with brown. More snow would be on the way soon. Megan wrapped her arms around her middle as she waited for the truck to warm. She swallowed a few times, blinking rapidly but not saying a word. An uneasy feeling dipped inside him.

"Can I bring over some dinner later?" he asked.

Megan sighed and shook her head. "No, thank you. I think I just want to be alone tonight."

Ice cut into Noah's gut; the feeling of unease he'd been pushing away for the past few hours grew in magnitude in his stomach.

"Sure," he said, steering down the familiar road to her apartment building before pulling into a parking space at the curb. Megan glanced over at the familiar building, pushing open the door before Noah had a chance to come around and open it for her. He met her at the lip of the curb.

"Will you be all right tonight?" he asked as he walked her to the front door of her building. She nodded, rubbing her hands rapidly together as if trying to scrub some warmth into them. He took her hands into his, sliding one glove on each.

"There, they'll be warm now."

Megan finally met his gaze, and he felt something stall in his chest. He couldn't decipher all the emotions lingering in her eyes, apart from the pain that seemed to glow like fire there. He silently berated himself for this uneasy emotion. Megan was grieving. It hurt him to see how much the loss of Mr. Ambrose was affecting her, and he wished there was some way he could take her pain.

"I'll see you tomorrow," he said quietly, bending down and kissing her cheek. He lingered there a moment, taking in her scent and the feel of her soft skin. Maybe he imagined it, but he was sure Megan had leaned in closer. Before he could fully comprehend the feeling, she had disappeared into her building, nixing the chance for him to remind her how much he loved her.

Noah stood for a long moment staring at the closed door, wondering before climbing into his truck and heading home. The night was on its way and the sky a dark blanket of stars. For once, there was no cloud cover; and the celestial beauty of God's creation could be seen in all its glory. If only he was in a better frame of mind to appreciate it.

He drove halfway down the main road back to his cottage, neck tight with anxiety, jaw set in frustration, when something made him pull to the side of the road. He parallel-parked his truck in front of Lana's bookstore and turned off the engine. He rested his hand on the door handle ready to climb out; maybe the cold air would drive some sense into him.

He paused. Listened. Feeling a bit like a crazy person, he blew out a heavy breath and rubbed his hand down his face, his rough five o' clock shadow scrapping his fingers. *Go back.* Noah leaned back heavily into the headrest and closed his eyes. What was he doing? The nagging feeling that he should turn around and return to Megan would not leave him. Everything in him wanted to go, but she didn't want him there. Hadn't she made that very clear when she had told him to leave her alone earlier? And yet the feeling still beat inside him.

The longer he sat in the truck staring at nothing, the stronger the feeling became. Megan needed him; and despite the possibility of her rejection, he was going to be there for her. There had been many times he had missed the cues with Teneal; and looking back now, he could see them appearing like signs spelling the disaster ahead. But this time he would be different; he would listen.

Sighing, he gave into the inevitable. *Okay, you better know what you are doing,* he silently said to the voice. Turning on the engine, he did a wide turn, pointing the truck in the direction of Megan's apartment complex, praying that he was doing the right thing.

Chapter Twenty-Seven

She'd barely held it together. Megan hurried into her apartment, slamming the door behind her and flinging herself onto her sofa. Pain like a thunderbolt thrummed through Megan's chest, and she curled into herself against it. Again—how could she live through this pain again? Despite her foreknowledge, the agony she felt could only be summed up in one word: all-encompassing. Not only was she dealing with the passing of Mr. Ambrose, but all the pain she still carried from the loss of her own parents also seemed to magnify her current grief.

She gasped in another breath, trying without success to draw in enough oxygen into her lungs to stop the tearing sensation inside her chest, to soothe it somehow. It didn't help. She'd held on as long as she could. Slowly, she burrowed her face into the sofa. Curling her arms around her chest, she gave into the torrent raging inside her. It hurt; oh, how it hurt. The tears did little to make the pain cease.

Somewhere in the distance, her phone rang again and again. She ignored it, too caught up in the pain wetting her flushed cheeks. In the haze, she heard a door open; the river of tears falling from her blurred her sight. She didn't have time to wonder, didn't have time to fear as warm, strong arms wrapped around her, drawing her closer into a very solid chest. Soft flannel scrubbed her cheeks, and she leaned into it. His scent was familiar and comforting, his body warm. The arms around her tightened as the torrent hit her wave after wave, sweeping over her and carrying her with the never-ending ebb and flow of her grief.

"Shhhh," Noah said. "I've got you, Megan." He whispered the words over and over and over again. Their sureness brought her comfort inside the storm, his warmth driving away the cold that had overtaken her body.

She held on for dear life. Moments, seconds, or days passed until slowly, the storm withdrew enough to release her. She felt him wrapped all around her like a downy blanket. Sometime during her avalanche of grief, he had laid down on the couch beside her, drawing her into his arms. He ran his calloused, gentle hands along her back until their slow, steady rhythm soothed her to calm.

Swallowing, she lay for a moment, breathing and thinking over the last few hours, listening to the steady beat of his heart. Megan didn't need to ask why Noah was there; she was just grateful he was.

"Noah, I—" She started to say.

Noah leaned down and slowly pressed his lips to hers.

"Its okay. I understand," he said quietly as he withdrew, pressing her head gently back into his shoulder and wrapping his arms around her, holding her close. "When I first got the news of Teneal's death, I didn't want to be near anyone either." He nuzzled into her hair. "I tried to let you be." He kissed her forehead, and she could hear his deep inhale. "I don't know what made me turn around and come back; but something told me I needed to be here, that you needed someone." Noah chuckled. "Levi would say it was a nudging of the Holy Spirit. Whatever it was, I am glad I listened."

Megan lifted her head, meeting his intense gaze, marveling again at the love she saw in depths of his eyes. "Me, too," she whispered.

The realization of something sweet, hopeful, and filled with joy entered her when she leaned back into Noah's strength, closing her eyes. *You are loved. I will be your Father, my child.*

Pushing them into a more seated position, Noah set her gently away from him and studied her face. "Are you okay?" he asked, staring at her tear-stained face. "I know there is nothing I can say that will make this feel any better, but I want you to know I am here for you—no matter what." He leaned in, gently pressing his lips to her, so quickly that she curled her hand around the back of his neck and pulled him to her again. He kissed her, tenderly, sweetly. This was not like the other passionate kisses they had shared; it was one that said he loved her, cared for her, and shared her pain.

She wanted to press for more; but as soon as she tried to deepen the kiss, Noah pulled away, drawing her into his chest again. "Let's save that for another time when we are not so emotional."

She sniffed, knowing he was right, over emotional moments and passion did not make a good end result. Noah chuckled, drawing her closer into this chest.

"What do you want for dinner?" he asked.

"I'm not really hungry." Her stomach growled, confuting her words.

"Really? So, a hot meaty pizza doesn't sound appetizing at all?" he teased.

Her stomach rumbled again. Noah grinned, fishing his phone from his back pocket and opening the Papa Paulo's app, quickly ordering two pizzas for delivery. While they waited, she rested in Noah's arms, enjoying the company; the feeling of not being alone; and most of all, the sureness of his love. Her phone rang again.

She looked at it for a long moment. Noah reached around her and answered the call.

"Hi, Tyreke. Yes, I am here, and Megan is okay." He wove his fingers in and out of hers as he listened to whatever her brother said next.

"Sure, I'll tell her. Good night."

"What did Tyreke say?" she asked, once Noah had ended the call.

"He wanted me to remind you that you have a family who loves you and are there for you."

Megan swallowed back a wad of emotion in her throat. In her heart, she knew she was loved; the trouble came when she wanted to lean in on that love.

"You don't have to be the strong one all the time, Megan," Noah said softly, placing a soft kiss on her forehead. "It's okay to let someone carry you sometimes."

A week later, Megan learned Noah's words to her were true. It was the day of the memorial service, and she desperately needed someone to carry her. Snowy Springs Community Church was solemn as the packed service began. Rows and rows of people who loved the Ambrose family filled the church, spilling into the entrance foyer at the back. Megan swallowed hard, squeezing tightly to the hand that steadily wrapped around her hand. Noah's other arm curved comfortably over the back of her.

She leaned into his side. It was a strange feeling not having to be the one who was strong for everyone else. The loss of George Ambrose had given her a much needed kick to realizing that she didn't have to be one who always said yes. She didn't have to put herself behind everyone else. As much as her family needed her, it was okay for her to need them, too. It was a hard lesson and one she no doubt would continue to learn as the days went on.

The service began, the piano striking up the first strains of "Count Your Blessings." Mrs. Ambrose had chosen the song.

"George is healed," she'd said. "Sometimes, the Lord answers our prayers in ways we don't expect. It is for our good and His glory. George is home, and I will miss him until I join him again in Heaven." A wide smile had broken over her face then. "I can have peace knowing that there will be a reunion one day between us."

Megan glanced to her side where Amana sat hemmed in by Tyreke and Mia, little Isaiah on her lap. Tears ran freely down her face; despite her pain, she smiled and sang along with the words. Megan sang along, stumbling over the words as her emotions rose. She wiped at her eyes. *Goodbye, George Ambrose, and thank you*, she thought, knowing that there would be moments she would be strong and others where the grief would hit her a fresh. It was the process she would go through.

This time, it was different; this time, she was not alone. Yes, she had Noah—and how she loved the man—however, she had something far greater than human love, the love of George Ambrose's Savior, the One she now called her own.

The singing and eulogies came to an end; and the pastor dismissed the service, the ushers wheeling the coffin out into the waiting hearse. It was sunny, bright rays bouncing off the white mountains of snow. The air was cold and freshly smelled of pine and open air. Her heart lifted, brightening the sorrow she'd felt during the memorial service.

"Are you okay?" Noah asked, leaning close to her ear, sending an unintended shiver down her spine.

She nodded, smiling, gratified by the smile she received in return. "Yes, I think I am."

Noah placed a warm hand at the small of her back, allowing her to precede him out of the building. He was a firm, sure presence behind her, lending her strength. There would be no graveside service. Mr. Ambrose had wanted to be cremated.

Leading her to the waiting reception hall, Noah stopped for her a moment, turned her to him, and hugged her close. She sagged into him enjoying, the solid strength he offered on such a difficult day.

"Ready to face the reception?" he asked.

She nodded.

Epilogue

The snow held off for the most stunning winter wedding Megan had ever seen. Snowy Springs Community Church glowed with the light of a thousand fairy lights scattered like stars around the main church building, where the happy couple said their vows and united as man and wife. The soft strains of the wedding march started up.

Megan looked over her shoulder, smiling as she saw her friend following Brady, the bride's nephew-in-law, suspended on unsteady legs between Mom Susie and Dad Ben. He babbled happily as Susie handed him another handful of lilac petals to scatter. Sarah, radiant in a fairy tale wedding dress, beamed. Her long, dark hair was suspended in a simple updo, her eyes focused only on one thing: Michael waiting at the end of the aisle.

The day was blessed with clear, sunny skies and slightly warmer than seasonal temperatures. Even so, the tenderness of the obvious love between bride and groom was what really kept the attendants' hearts warm. Megan's gaze shifted to her left, sweeping over the Thomas side of the wedding. Noah stood breathtakingly handsome in a dark suit, white shirt, and blue tie beside his brothers. He looked back, meeting her gaze as the minister began to read the traditional wedding vows for Michael and Sarah to repeat. He raised an eyebrow, smiled, and lifted his left hand, pointing to the ring finger and then to her. A giddiness fluttered in her chest, knowing that one day soon, it would be their turn. In an unexpected turn of events, Noah had asked her to marry him while they took a walk in between the pine Christmas trees on Buck's farm.

"This is where the trees are planted until they mature enough to be sold at market. Afterward, we take them there for baling, sanitizing, and packaging," he said, taking her one hand in his and leading her to a barn with a complicated set of machines waiting inside. When they entered, Noah stood beside a barrel, looking down and smiling.

"What?" she asked.

"At the risk of sounding really sentimental, this was where I made the decision to take a chance with you," he said softly, drawing her into his chest. "I was so unsure with you. Did I risk making the same mistakes again or even new ones, or did I let the past stay in the past and try to make a relationship with you the best I could?"

"What made you decide it was worth it?" she asked, curious to know what Noah had been thinking.

"I imagined my life without you," he said so earnestly, her breath caught in her chest. "I didn't like the thought of it." He pulled her tighter to him. "You bring me joy, Megan Davis; and one day, when both of us are ready, we can talk about what the future holds." He lost his grip on her.

Megan caught his hands and wrapped them around her waist, pressing up for a kiss. Noah obliged; and the familiar tickle of flames raced through her veins, causing warmth to spill all over her body. Once they parted, she didn't understand why Noah had let go of her and stepped back; but soon enough, she did.

"Megan Davis, I know we've only been together for a short time. I love you with everything in me. Will you marry me?"

He looked so handsome and hopeful—and her heart was so full—she couldn't give any other answer than yes.

"Enjoying the wedding?" Noah asked, coming to stand beside her, bringing her back to the present. He leaned down, kissing her cheek, his mouth lingering on her skin.

"I would have liked it here," she said, smiling wide and pointing to her mouth. Heat rose in her cheeks, and she could feel it beaming out as a knowing smile slid over Noah's gorgeous mouth.

"In that case . . . " He brought his face closer to hers, dropping a sweet and hard kiss on her upturned lips. Megan knew she shouldn't, but the feel of his mouth against hers distracted her thoroughly. She tucked her fingers into the lapels of his dress jacket and held him there, unwilling to let him get away so easily.

Noah didn't need another invitation; his mouth pressed more firmly against hers, hands gripping her waist in a kiss that was rapidly going beyond what was proper in company, although might not be out of place at a wedding. As it had turned out, the discussion about the future had happened a lot sooner than either of them had anticipated.

"Get a room, you two," Tyreke said, laughing, gesturing to the stunned faces of Noah's mother and Lana.

Megan blushed as Noah enfolded her into his chest; she could feel the warm rumble of his laughter in his chest pressed firmly against her.

"Don't I wish," Noah muttered for her ears alone.

The heat in her face reached volcanic warmth; and she swatted him across the chest, leaning back to better see his face. "Noah."

"What? Like the whole world doesn't know how much I would like the next few weeks to pass as quickly as possible."

"You only asked me to marry you two weeks ago. I think six weeks to plan our wedding is a really short time to wait." She laughed as he leaned down to kiss her again. This time, after one, she pushed back, placing plenty of well-needed space between them.

"Not if we go to Vegas and elope."

She almost caved at the hopeful look on his face. When Noah had first proposed, she'd been worried about what kind of wedding they would have. After all, it was her first wedding and his second; but as Noah had slid his ring onto her finger and kissed all good sense from her, she'd come to realize that as long as they had each other and God, it didn't matter.

"I love you, Noah Thomas, but there is no way we are going to Vegas to get married; and you know it."

Noah's face softened, his laughing expression fading into tenderness so sweet, she felt her toes curl and wondered how she had been so incredibly lucky to be with a man like him, "And I love you, Megan Davis. As long as I get to marry you, that is all that matters."

He took her hand in his, gently leading her out of the banquet hall to a place they wouldn't have an audience, and pulled her firmly against his chest. His mouth came down onto hers again. This kiss was different; it was a confirmation, a message, and it was overflowing with joy. It was his love for her pouring out in each sweep of his mouth.

When they parted, breathing hard, Noah held her, one arm around her waist and the other drawing lazy sweeps up and down her arm.

"Just for the record," he said, "I can't wait to be your husband."

She linked her arms around his neck, drawing his mouth to hers again. Before she kissed him, she whispered, "No more than I can wait to be your wife."

Leading her back into the hall where Michael and Sarah had begun their first dance, Noah turned her in his arms and slowly danced her onto the floor. Drawing her close and nuzzling into her hair, he sighed with contentment. She couldn't remember the last time she had felt this happy, this loved, and finally the peace she'd wanted for so long. Death didn't scare her anymore, and her future looked beautiful.

About the Author

Michelle Dykman is a reader, teacher, and debut author of *You, Me and the Stars*. After spending ten years crunching numbers, Michelle discovered her two true passions, teaching and writing clean and wholesome Christian romance novels for adults and teens. Michelle has a teaching degree and has spent many years enjoying the works of other Christian authors which spurred on her passion for writing memorable novels. Her teen books are written from a background of teaching and working with teens for many years and a heart for them to live full and regret-free lives. Michelle lives with her husband and two boys in the snowy and sometimes hot areas of Canada and from time to time misses the dry warmth of her home country, South Africa.

For more information about
Michelle Dykman
&
All I Want for Christmas
please visit:

www.michelledykman.com

For more information about
AMBASSADOR INTERNATIONAL
please visit:

www.ambassador-international.com

When Lena Neubauer is sent from Germany to America to help her immigrant brother on his farm and with his young children, she never expects what awaits her in antebellum America. With family honor and devotion propelling her across to an unknown world, Lena soon finds herself stepping into this strange world. After tragedy strikes, Lena finds herself finally at the crossroads and must make a decision that will affect her future—and her family's future—forever.

Rob Wilkinson, a Christian man from Northern Ireland and an avid world traveler in his spare time, finds himself traveling alone on the second anniversary of his wife's untimely death. But through a couple of seeming coincidences, he meets and befriends Gabby, a young woman from Germany dealing with heartaches of her own. As their relationship deepens, Rob must draw on his recently-tested faith to help Gabby overcome her own lapsed faith in God and find a new life beyond her pain.

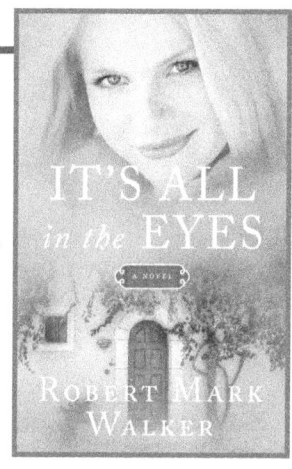

Julie loves her husband, Eric, but being a military wife is lonely. Julie finds herself going out for a night, where she meets Matt. On the other side of the ocean, Eric is missing his family. One of his fellow servicemen, Cal, is different. He claims Jesus has made an impact on his life, but Eric isn't sure if that's the companionship he needs right now. He's a soldier, after all, and he deserves to have a little fun. But one bad decision leads to another and another, and Julie and Eric both find themselves lost and searching for . . . something or Someone.